STRAP DOWN!

Travis grabbed at the protecting bands on his chair. The ship no longer felt inert and drifting—she was coming alive . . . Travis lay back, watching the vision plate. Now that the brighter glare of the sun was gone he could pick up a smaller dot, far smaller than the star which nurtured it.

"Something tells me, boy," Renfry said in a small and hesitant voice, "that's where we're going."

"Earth?" A warm surge of hope spread through Travis.

"An earth maybe—but not ours."

ANDRE NORTON

GALACTIC DERELICT

ACE BOOKS, NEW YORK

GALACTIC DERELICT

An Ace Book / published by arrangement with
Philomel Books

PRINTING HISTORY
Ace edition / April 1972

ISBN: 0-441-27234-7

Ace Books are published by The Berkley Publishing Group,
200 Madison Avenue, New York, New York 10016.
The name "ACE" and the "A" logo
are trademarks belonging to Charter Communications, Inc.

PRINTED IN THE UNITED STATES OF AMERICA

10 9 8 7 6 5 4 3

HOT—it sure was stacking up to be a hot one today. He'd better check on the spring in the brakes before the sun really boiled up the country ahead. That was the only water in this whole frying pan of baking rock—or was it?

Travis Fox hitched forward in his saddle to study the pinkish yellow of the bare desert strip between him and that faint, distant line of green juniper against the buff of sagebrush which marked the cuts of the brakes. This was a barren land, forbidding to anyone not native to its harshness.

It was also a land in which time was frozen into one color-streaked mold of unchanging rock and earth, and in that it was probably now unique upon the rider's planet. Elsewhere around the world deserts had been flooded, through man's efforts, with sea water freed of its burden of salt. Ordered farms beat ancient sand dunes into dim memories. Mankind was fast becoming no longer subject to the whim of weather or climate. Yet here the free desert remained unaltered because the nation within which it lay was still rich enough not to need all of its soil under cultivation.

Someday this, too, would be swept away, taking with it the heritage of such as Travis Fox. For five hundred years, or perhaps close to a thousand now—no one could rightly say when the first Apache clan had come questing into this territory— these canyons and sand wastes, valleys and mesas had been dominated by a tough, desert-born breed who could travel and fight, and live off bleakness no other race dared face without supplies laboriously transported. His ancestors had waged war which lasted almost four centuries across this country. And now the survivors wrested a living from the same region with a like determination.

That spring in the brakes . . . Travis' brown fingers began to count off seasons in taps on his saddle horn. Nineteen . . . twenty . . . This was the twentieth year after the last big dry, and if Chato was right, that meant the water which should be there was due for a periodical failure. And the old man had been correct in his prediction of an unusually arid summer this year.

If Travis rode straight there to find the spring dry, he'd lose most of the day, and time was important. They *had* to move the breeding stock to a sure water supply. On the other hand if he cut back into the

2

Canyon of the Hohokam on just a hunch and was wrong—then Whelan would have every right to lay into him for being a fool. Whelan stubbornly refused to follow the Old Ones' knowledge. And in that his brother was himself a fool.

Travis laughed softly. The White-eyes—deliberately he used the old warrior's term for a traditional enemy, saying it aloud, "Pinda-lick-o-yi"—the White-eyes didn't know *everything*. And a few of them were willing to admit it once in a while.

Then he laughed again, this time at himself and his own thoughts. Scratch the rancher—and the Apache was right under the surface of his sun-dried hide. Only there was a bitter note in that second laugh and Travis booted his pinto into a lope with more force than was necessary. He didn't care to follow the trail of those particular thoughts. He'd make for the place of the Hohokam and he'd be Apache for today; there was nothing to spoil that as his other dreams had been spoiled.

Whelan thought that if an Apache lived like the White-eyes, and set aside all the old things, then he would gain all their advantages. To Whelan there was nothing good in the past, and even to consider the Old Ones, what they did and why they did it, was a foolish waste of time. Travis bit again on disappointment, to find it as fresh and bad-tasting as it had been a year earlier.

The pinto threaded a way between boulders along the course of a dried stream bed. Odd that a land now so arid could carry so many signs of past water. There were miles of irrigation ditches used by the Old Ones, marking the sun-baked pans of open land

3

which had not known the touch of moisture for centuries. Travis urged his mount up a sharp slope and headed west, feeling the heat bore into his straight back through the single layer of faded shirt fabric.

He doubted if Whelan knew of the Canyon of the Hohokam. That was one of the things from the old days, a story preserved by such as Chato. And there were now two kinds of Apache—Chato and Whelan. Chato denied the existence of the White-eyes, living his own life behind a shutter which he dropped between him and the outside world, the world of the whites. And Whelan denied the existence of the Apache, being all white with an effort.

Once Travis had seen a third way, that of bending the white man's learning to blend with Apache lore. He thought he had discovered those who agreed with him. But it had all gone, as quickly as a drop of water poured upon rock surface here would vanish. Now he tended to agree with Chato—and, knowing that, Chato had freely given him information Whelan did not have, facts concerning Whelan's own range land.

Chato's father—again Travis counted, fingertip against saddle horn—why, Chato's father would be a hundred and twenty years old if he were alive today! And he had been born in the Hohokam's valley while his family were hiding out from the blue-coated soldiers.

Chato had known of the lost canyon, had guided Travis to it when he was so small he could barely grip a horse's barrel with his short legs. And he had returned there again and again through the years.

The houses of the Hohokam had intrigued him, and the spring there never failed. There were piñons with a rich harvest of nuts to be gathered in season, and some stunted fruit trees still yielding a measure of fruit. Once it had been a garden; now it was a hidden oasis.

Travis was working his way into the maze of canyons which held the forgotten trail of the Old Ones when he heard that hum. Out of the instinct he drew rein, knowing that he was in the concealing shadow of a cliff wall, and glanced skyward.

"'Copter!" He said it aloud in sheer surprise. The ageless desert country had claimed him so thoroughly during the past few hours that sighting that very modern mode of travel came almost as a shock.

Could it be Whelan, checking up on him? Travis' mouth tightened. But when he had left the ranch house at sunup, Bill Redhorse, Chato's grandson, had been working on the engine of the ranch bus. Anyway, Whelan couldn't waste fuel on desert coasting. With the big war scare on again, rationing had tightened up and a man kept his 'copter for emergencies, working horses again for daily work.

The war scare . . . Travis thought about it as he watched the strange machine out of sight. Ever since he could remember there had been snapping and snarling in the newspapers, on the radio, on the TV screen. Little scrimmages bursting out, smoldering, talk and more talk. Then, some months back, something queer had happened in Europe—a big blast set off in the north. Though the Reds had not explained what had happened and clamped down tight all their

5

screen of secrecy, rumor had it that some kind of a new bomb had gone wrong. All this might be only preliminary to an out-and-out break between East and West.

And the VIPs chose to believe that was true. There was a tightening up of regulations all along the line, a whispering of trouble to come. New fuel rationing slapped on, a tenseness in the air . . .

Out here it was easy enough to shove all that stuff out of one's mind. The desert dried out to nothing the bickering of men. These cliffs had stood the same before the brown-skinned men of his race had trickled down from the north. They would probably be standing, though perhaps radioactive, when the White-eyes blasted both white and brown men out of it again.

The sight of the 'copter had triggered memories Travis did not like. He continued to wonder, as the machine disappeared in the direction he himself was following, what its mission was here.

He did not sight it again, which strengthened his belief that the machine carried no local rancher. If the pilot had been hunting herd strays, he would circle. Prospectors? But there had been no news of a government expedition, and during the past five years prospecting had been rigidly controlled.

Travis located the concealed turn-off into the hidden canyon. As the pinto picked a careful way, his rider studied the ground. There was no sign that any man had passed that way for a long time. He clicked his tongue and the horse quickened pace. They had gone perhaps two miles along that snake's path when Travis brought his mount to a halt.

The warning had been borne by a puff of breeze tickling his nose. This was no desert wind laden with heat and grit, for it carried the scent of juniper. The pinto nickered and mouthed its bit—water ahead. But also the land before them was not empty of men.

Travis swung out of the saddle, taking his rifle with him. Unless the past year had seen some changes in the terrain ahead, there was a good cover on the lip of the hidden canyon's entrance. Without being visible himself, he would be able to survey the camp therein. For camp smells reached him now—wood smoke, coffee, frying bacon.

The ascent to his chosen spy post was easy. From below came the pine scent, heavier now, drawn out by the sun's rays, and the small, busy twittering of birds about their own concerns. There was a cup of green lying there, about a spring-fed pool which mirrored the hot blue of the sky. Between that water and the vast shallow cave which held the block city of the Old Ones, stood the 'copter. And tending a cooking fire was a man. A second had gone to the pool for water.

Travis did not believe they were ranchers. But they wore the sturdy clothing of outdoor men and moved about the business of making camp with assurance. He began to inventory what he could see of their supplies and equipment.

The 'copter was of the latest model. And in the shade offered by a small stand of trees he could make out bedrolls. But he did not sight any digging tools, any indication that this was a prospecting team. Then the man walked back from the pool, set his filled bucket down by the fire, and dropped crosslegged before a big package which he proceeded to free from a canvas covering. Travis watched him uncover what could only be a portable communicator of advanced design.

The operator was patiently inching the antenna rod up into the air, when Travis heard the pinto nicker. Age-old instinct he was not conscious of brought him around, still on his knees, with rifle ready. But it was only to front another weapon with a deadly promise in the open mouth of the barrel aimed directly and mercilessly at his middle.

Above that unwavering gunsight, gray eyes watched him with a chill detachment worse than any vocal threat. Travis Fox considered himself a worthy descendant of generations of the toughest warriors this stretch of country had ever seen. Yet he knew that neither he nor any of his kind had ever before faced a man quite like this one. And this man was young, no older than himself, so that that subtle menace did not altogether fit with the lithe, slender body or that calm, boyish face.

"Drop it!" The man delivered his order with the authority of one expecting no resistance. Travis did just that, allowing the rifle to slip from his hands and slide across his leg to the gravel of the hillside.

"On your feet. Make it snappy. Down there. . . ." The stream of orders issued in a gentle voice and even tone, both of which oddly increased the menace Travis sensed.

He stood up, turned downslope and walked forward, his hands up, palms out, at shoulder level. What he had stumbled on here he did not know, but that it was important—and dangerous—Travis did not doubt.

The man who was cooking and the man at the com set both sat back on their heels to survey him calmly as he advanced, the high heels of his boots acting as brakes on the slope. To his eyes they were little different from the white ranchers he knew in the district. Yet the cook . . .?

Travis studied him, puzzled certain that he had seen the man or his likeness before under very different circumstances.

"Where did you flush this one, Ross?" asked the man at the com.

"Lying up on the ridge, getting an eyeful," Travis' captor replied with his usual economy of words.

The cook stood up, wiped his hands on a cloth, and started toward them. He was the eldest of the three strangers, his skin deeply tanned, his eyes a startlingly bright blue against that brown. He carried with him an authority which did not suit his present employment but which marked him, for Travis, as the leader of the party. The Apache guessed his own reception would depend upon this man's reaction. Only why did some faint twist of memory persist in outlining the cook's head with a black square?

Since the stranger seemed to be in no hurry to ask questions, Travis met him eye to eye, drawing on his own brand of patience. There was danger in this man, too, the same controlled force which had moved the youngster when he trapped the Apache on the heights.

"Apache." It was a statement, rather than a question. And it added a bit to Travis' estimation of the stranger. There were few men nowadays who took the trouble, or had the real knowledge necessary, to distinguish Apache from Hopi, Navajo, or Ute in one brief glance.

"Rancher?" That was a question this time and Travis gave it a truthful answer. He had a growing conviction that to use any evasive tactics with this particular White-eye would not lead to anything but his own disadvantage.

"Rider for the Double A."

The man by the com unit had unrolled a map. Now he ran a forefinger along an uneven marking and nodded, not at Travis, but to the interrogator.

"Nearest range to the east. But he can't be hunting strays this far into the desert."

"Good water." The other nodded at the pool. "The Old Ones used it."

Obliquely that was another inquiry. And somehow Travis found himself replying to it.

"The Old Ones knew. Not those only." With his chin he pointed to the ruins in the great shallow cave. "But the People in turn. Never dry, even in bad years."

"And this is a bad year." The stranger rubbed his hand along his jaw, his blue eyes still holding Travis'. "A complication we didn't forsee. So Double A runs a herd in here in dry years, son?"

Again Travis found himself, against his will replying with the exact truth. "Not yet. Few of the riders know of it now. Not many care to listen to the stories of the old men." He was still puzzling over the teasing memory of seeing this man's lean face before. That black border about it—a frame! A picture frame! And the picture had hung over Dr. Morgan's desk at the university.

"But you do. . . ." There came another of those measuring stares like the one which had stripped the rancher's clothing from him to display the Apache underneath. Now those eyes might be trying to sort out the thoughts in his head. Dr. Morgan's study— this man's picture—but with a stepped pyramid behind him.

"It is so." Absently he used another speech pattern as he tried to remember more.

"The problem is, buster"—the man by the com unit stood up, spoke lazily— "just what are we going to do with you now? How about it, Ashe? Does he go in cold storage—maybe up there?" He jerked a thumb at the ruins.

Ashe! Dr. Gordon Ashe! He'd put a name to the stranger at last. And with the name he had a reason for the man's presence there. Ashe was an archaeologist. Only Travis did not have to look at the com unit or at the camp to guess that this was no expedition to hunt relics of ancient man. He had had firsthand knowledge of those. What were Dr. Ashe and his companions doing in the Canyon of the Dead?

"You can put down your hands, son," Dr. Ashe said. "And you can make it easy for yourself if you agree to stay here peaceably for a time."

"For how long?" countered Travis.

"That depends," Ashe hedged.

"I left my horse up there. He needs water."

"Bring the horse down, Ross."

Travis turned his head. The young man holstered his odd-looking weapon and climbed upslope, to reappear shortly leading the pinto. Travis freed his mount of saddle and turned the animal loose. He came back to the camp site to find Ashe awaiting him.

"So not many people know of this place?"

Travis shrugged. "One other man on the Double A—he is very old. His father was born here, long ago when the Apaches were fighting the army. Nobody else is interested any more."

"Then there was never any digging done in the ruins?"

"A little—once."

"By whom?"

Travis pushed back his hat. "Me." His answer was short, antagonistic.

"Oh?" Ashe produced a package of cigarettes, offered them. Travis took one without thinking.

"You came here for a dig?" he counter-questioned.

"In a manner of speaking." But when Ashe glanced at the cliff house, Travis thought it was as if he saw something far more interesting behind or beyond those crumbling blocks of sun-dried brick.

"I thought your main interest was pre-Mayan, Dr. Ashe." Travis squatted on his heels, brought out a smoldering twig from the fire to light his smoke, and was inwardly satisfied to note that he had at last startled the archaeologist with that observation.

"You know me!" He made a challenge of the words.

Travis shook his head. "I know Doctor Prentiss Morgan."

"So that's it! You're one of his bright boys!"

"No." That was short, a bitten-off warning not to probe. And the other man must have been sensitive enough to understand at once, for he asked no other question.

"Chow ready, Ashe?" asked the man with the com. Behind him the youngster Ashe called "Ross" came to the fire, reached out for the frying pan. Travis stared at his hand. The flesh was seamed with scars and once before the Apache had seen healed wounds like those—from a deep and painful burn. He looked away hurriedly as the other apportioned food onto plates, and he got his own lunch from his saddlebags.

They ate in silence, an oddly companionable silence. The tension of the first minutes of their meeting eased from the range rider. His interest in these men, his desire to know more about them and what they were doing here, dampened his annoyance at the way he had been captured. That young Ross was a slick tracker. He must have had experience at such games to trap Travis so neatly. The Apache longed for a closer look at the other's weapon. He was certain it was not a conventional revolver. And the very fact that Ross wore it ready for use argued that he was on guard against expected attack.

There was a difference between Ashe and Ross, and the man operating the com, which became plainer the longer Travis studied the three covertly. Ashe and Ross might be of a different breed from the third man. Their alikeness went deeper than just their heavy tans, their silent walk, their watchfulness and complete awareness of their surroundings. The more Travis watched them absorbed as they were in the very natural business of eating and then policing camp, the more sure he was that they had *not* come to this place to explore cliff ruins, that they were engaged in some more serious and perhaps deadly action.

He asked no questions, content to let the others now make the first move. It was the com unit which broke the peace of the small camp. A warning cackle brought its tender on the run. He snapped on earphones and then relayed a message.

"Procedure has to be stepped up. They'll start bringing the stuff in tonight!"

2

"WELL?" Ross's glance swept over Travis, settled on Ashe.

"Anybody know you were coming here?" the older man asked the range rider.

"I came out to check all the springs. If I don't return to the ranch within a reasonable time, they'll hunt me up, yes." Travis saw no reason to enlarge upon that with two other bits of information. One, that Whelan would not be unduly alarmed if he did not return within twenty-four hours, and the other that he was supposed to be in the brakes to the south.

"You say that you know Prentiss Morgan—how well?"

"I was in one of his classes at the U—for a while."

"Your name?"

"Fox. Travis Fox."

The com operator cut in, again consulting his map. "The Double A belongs to a Fox—"

"My brother. But I work for him, that's all."

"Grant"—Ashe turned now to the com man—"mark this top priority and send it to Kelgarries. Ask him to check Fox—all the way."

"We can ship him out when the first load comes in, chief. They will store him at headquarters as long as you want," Ross offered, as if Travis had ceased to be a person and was now only an annoying problem.

Ashe shook his head. "Look here, Fox, we don't want to make it hard for you. It's pure bad luck that you trailed in here today. Frankly, we can't afford to attract any attention to our activities at present. But if you'll give me your word not to try and go over the hill, we'll leave it at that for the present."

The last thing Travis wanted to do was leave. His curiosity was thoroughly aroused, and he had no intention of going unless they removed him bodily. And that, he promised himself silently, would take a lot of doing.

"It's a deal."

But Ashe was already on another track. "You say you did some digging over there. What did you uncover?"

"The usual stuff—pottery, a few arrowheads. The site is probably pre-Columbian. These mountains are filled with such ruins."

"What did you expect, chief?" Ross asked.

"Well, there was a slim chance," the other returned ambiguously. "This climate preserves. We've found baskets, fabrics, fragile things lasting—"

"I'll take the bones and baskets—in place of some other things." Ross held his scarred hand against his chest and rubbed its seamed flesh with the other, as if soothing a wound which still ached. "Better get out the lights if the boys are going to drop in tonight."

The pinto continued to graze in the center of the meadow while Ross and Ashe paced out two lines and spaced small plastic canisters at intervals. Travis, watching, guessed they were marking a landing site. But it was twice the size needed by a 'copter such as the one now standing beyond. Then Ashe settled with his back against a tree, reading the leaves of a bulging notebook, while Ross brought out a roll of felt and opened it.

What he uncovered was a set of five stone points, beautifully fashioned, too long to be arrowheads. And Travis recognized their distinctive shape, the pattern of those flaked edges! Far better workmanship than the later productions of his own people, yet much older. He had held their like in his hands, admired the artistry of the forgotten weapon maker who had patiently chipped them into being. Folsom points! They were intended to head the throwing spears of men who went up so equipped against mammoth, giant bison, cave bear, and Alaskan lion.

"Folsom man here?" He saw Ross glance toward him, Ashe's attention lift from the notebook.

Ross picked up the last point in that row held it

out to Travis. He took it carefully. The head was perfect, fine. He turned it over between his fingers and then paused—not sure of what he knew, or why.

"Fake."

Yet was it? He had handled Folsom points and some, in spite of their great age, had been as perfectly preserved as this one. Only—this did not feel right. He could give no better reason for his judgment than that.

"What makes you think so?" Ashe wanted to know.

"That one was certified by Stefferds." Ross took up the second point from the line. But Travis, instead of being confounded by that certification from the authority on prehistoric American remains, remained sure of his own appraisal.

"Not the right feel to it."

Ashe nodded to Ross, who picked up a third stone head, offering it in exchange for the one Travis still held. The new point was, to all examination by eye, a copy of the first. Yet, as he ran a forefinger along the fine serrations of the flaked edge, Travis knew that this was the real thing, and he said so.

"Well, well." Ross studied his store of points. "Something new had been added," he informed the empty space before him.

"It's been done before," Ashe said. "Give him your gun."

For a moment it seemed as if Ross might refuse, and he frowned as he drew the weapon. The Apache, putting down the Folsom point with care, took the weapon and examined it closely. Though its general shape was that of a revolver, there were enough differences to make it totally new to Travis. He sighted it at a tree trunk and found that when it was held correctly for firing, the grip was not altogether comfortable, as if the hand for which it had been fashioned was not quite like his own.

There was another difference growing in his mind the longer he held the weapon. He did not like that odd sensation. . . .

Travis laid the gun down beside the flint point, regarding them both with wide and astonished eyes. From them he had gained a common impression of age—a wide expanse of time separating him from the makers of those two very disimilar weapons. For the Folsom point that feeling was correct. But why did the gun give him the same answer? He had come to rely on that queer unnamed sense of his—its apparent failure now was disconcerting.

"How old is the gun?" asked Ashe.

"It can't be—" Travis protested against the verdict of his sense. "I won't believe that it is as old—or older—than the spearhead!"

"Brother"—Ross regarded him with an odd expression—"you can call 'em!" He reholstered the gun. "So now we have a time guesser, chief."

"Such a gift is not too uncommon," Ashe commented absently. "I've seen it in operation before."

"But a gun can't *be* that old!" Travis still objected. Ross's left eyebrow raised in a sardonic arc as he gave a half-smile.

"That's all you know about it, brother," he observed. "New recruit?" That was addressed to

Ashe. The latter was frowning, but at Ross's inquiry he smiled with a warmth which for a second or two made Travis uncomfortable. It so patently advertised that those two were a long-established team, shutting him outside.

"Don't rush things, boy." Ashe stood up and went over to the com unit. "Any news from the front?"

"Cackle-cackle, yacketty-yak," snorted the operator. "Soon as I tune out one band interference, we hit another. Someday maybe they'll make these walkie-talkies so they'll really operate without over-loading a guy's eardrums. No, nothing for us yet."

Travis wanted to ask questions, a lot of them. But he was also sure that most would receive evasive answers. He tried to fit the gun into the rest of his jigsaw of surmises, hints, and guesses, and found it wouldn't. But he forgot that when Ashe sat down once more and began to talk archaeologist's shop. At first Travis only listened, then he realized he was being drawn more and more into answering, into giving opinions and once or twice daring to contradict the other. Apache lore, cliff ruins, Folsom man—Ashe's conversation ranged widely. It was only after Travis had been led to talking freely with the pent-up eagerness of one who has been denied expression for too long, that he understood the other man must have been testing his knowledge in the field.

"Sounds rugged, the way they lived then," Ross observed at the conclusion of Travis' story of the use of their present camp site by Apache holdouts in the old days.

"That, from you, is good," Grant said, laughing, and then snapped on his earphones once more as the com came to life. With one hand he steadied a pad on his knee and wrote in quick dashes.

Travis studied the shadows on the cliffs. It wasn't far from sundown now, and he was growing impatient. This was like being in a theater waiting for the curtain to go up—or lying in wait for trouble to come pounding around some bend when you had a rifle in hand.

Ashe took the scribbled page from Grant, checked it against more scribbles in his notebook. Ross was chewing on a long stem of grass, relaxed, outwardly almost sleepy. Yet Travis suspected that if he were to make a wrong move, Ross would come very wide awake in an instant.

"You know this country must have been popping once," Ross commented lazily. "That looks like a regular apartment house over there—with maybe a hundred, two hundred people living in it. How *did* they live, anyway? This is a small valley."

"There's another valley to the northwest with irrigation ditches still marked," Travis replied. "And they hunted—turkey, deer, antelope, even buffalo—if they were lucky."

"Now if a man had some way to look back into history he could learn a lot—"

"You mean by using an infra-red Vis-Tex?" Travis asked with careful casualness, and had the satisfaction of seeing the other's calm crack. Then he laughed, with an edge on his humor. "We Indians don't wear blankets or feathers in our hair any more, and some of us read and watch TV, and actually go

21

to school. But the Vis-Tex I saw in action wasn't too successful." He decided on a guess. "Planning to test a new model here?"

"In a way—yes."

Travis had not expected a serious answer like that. And it was Ashe who had made it, plainly to the surprise of Ross. But the possibilities opened up by that assent were startling.

Photographing the past, beginning with a few hours past, by the infra-red waves, had succeded in experimentation as far back as twenty years previously—during the late fifties. The process had been perfected to a point where objects would appear on films exposed a week after the disappearance of those objects from a given point. And Travis had been present on one occasion when an experimental Vis-Tex had been demonstrated by Dr. Morgan. But if they *did* have a new model which could produce a real reach back into history—! He drew a deep breath and stared at the cave-enclosed ruins before him. What would it mean to bring the past to visual life again! Then he grinned.

"A lot of history will have to be rewritten in a hurry if you have one that works."

"Not history as we know it." Ashe drew out cigarettes and passed them. "Son, you're a part of this now, whether or no. We can't afford to let you go, the situation is too critical. So—you'll be offered a chance to enlist."

"In what?" countered Travis warily.

"In Project Folsom One." Ashe lit his cigarette. "Headquarters checked you out all along the line.

22

I'm inclined to think that providence had a hand in your turning up here today. It all fits."

"Too well?" There was a frown line between Ross's brows.

"No," Ashe replied. "He's just what he said he is. Our man reported from the Double A and from Morgan. He can't be a plant."

What kind of a plant? wondered Travis. Apparently he was being drafted, but he wanted to know more about why and for what. He said so with determination and then believed he wasn't hearing correctly when Ashe answered.

"We're here to see the Folsom hunters' world."

"That's a tall order, Doctor Ashe. You've a super Vis-Tex if you can take a peek ten thousand years back."

"More likely farther than that," Ashe corrected him. "We aren't sure yet."

"Why the hush-hush? A look at some roaming primitive tribe should bring out the TV and the newsmen—"

"We're more interested in other things than primitive tribesmen."

"Such as where that gun came from," agreed Ross. He was again rubbing his scarred hand, and there was that in the bleakness of his eyes which Travis recognized from their first meeting on the rim of the canyon. It was the look of a fighter moving in to give battle.

"You'll have to take up on faith for a while," Ashe cut in. "This is a queer business and a necessarily top-secret one, to use the patter of our times."

They ate supper and Travis moved the pinto to the narrow lower end of the canyon, well away from the improvised landing field. Dusk had hardly closed in before the first of the cargo 'copters touched down. Soon he found himself making one of a line of men passing packages and boxes from the machine back to the shelter of the small grove of trees. They worked without any waste motion at a speed which suggested that time was of the highest importance, and Travis found that he had caught that need for haste from them. The first machine was stripped of its load, rose, and was gone only minutes before a second one came in to take its place. Again an unloading chain formed, this time for heavier boxes which required two men to handle them.

Travis' back ached, his hands were raw by the time the fourth 'copter was freed and left. Four more men had joined their party, one coming in with each load, but there was little talk. All were concentrating on the unloading and storing of the material. In a period of lull after the departure of the fourth machine, Ashe came up to Travis accompanied by another man.

"Here he is." Ashe's hand closed on Travis' shoulder, drawing him out to face the newcomer.

He was taller than Dr. Ashe, and there was no mistaking the air of command, or the power of those eyes which looked straight into the Apache. But after a long moment the big man smiled briefly.

"You're quite a problem for us, Fox."

"Or the missing ingredient," corrected Ashe. "Fox, this is Major Kelgarries, at present our commanding officer."

"We'll have a talk later," Kelgarries promised. "Tonight's rather busy."

"Clear the field!" called someone from the flare line. "Setting down."

They plunged out of the path of the fifth 'copter and work started again. The Major, Travis noted, was right in line with the others when it came to tossing boxes around, nor was there any more time for talking.

Seven or eight loads, which was it? Travis tried to count them up, wriggling stiff fingers. It was still night but the flares had been extinguished. The men who had worked together now sat around the fire drinking coffee and wolfing sandwiches which had been delivered with the last cargo. They did not talk much and Travis knew they were as tired as he was.

"Bedtime, brother. And am I glad to hit the sack!" Ross said between yawns. "Need the makings—blankets—anything?"

Half stupid with fatigue, Travis shook his head. "Got my bedroll with m'saddle." And he was asleep almost before he was fully stretched out on that limited comfort.

In the day light of morning the camp looked disorganized. But men were already at work sorting out the material, working as if this was a task they had often done before. Travis, helping to shift a large crate, looked up to see the Major.

"Spare me a moment, Fox." He led the way from the scene of activity.

"You've got yourself—and us—in a muddle, young man. Frankly, we can't turn you loose—for your own sake, as well as ours. This project has to be kept under wraps and there are some very tough boys who would like to pick you up and learn what they could from you. So, we either take you all the way in—or put you on ice. It's up to you which it is going to be. You've been vouched for by Doctor Morgan.''

Travis tensed. What had they raked up now? Memories pinched as might a too-tight cinch about the belly. But if they'd been asking questions of Prentiss Morgan, they must know what happened last year—and why. Apparently they did, for Kelgarries continued:

''Fox, the time when anyone can afford prejudices is past—way past. I know about Hewitt's offer to the University and what happened when he pressured to have you fired from the expedition staff. But prejudices can stretch both ways—you didn't stand up to him very long, did you?''

Travis shrugged. ''Maybe you've heard the term 'second-class citizen,' Major. How do you suppose Indians rate with some people in this country? To that crowd we are and we'll always be dirty, ignorant savages. You can't fight when the other fellow has all the weapons himself. Hewitt gave that grant to the University to do some important work. When he wanted me off, that was that. If I'd let Doctor Morgan fight to keep me on his staff, Hewitt would have snatched his check away again so fast the friction would have burnt the paper. I know Hewitt and what makes him tick. And Doctor Morgan's work was more important—'' Travis stopped short. Why in the world had he told the Major all that? It was none of

Kelgarries' business why he had quit and come back to the ranch.

"There aren't many like Hewitt left—fortunately. And I assure you we do not follow his methods. If you choose to join us after Ashe briefs you, you're one of a team. Lord, man"—the Major slapped his hand vigorously against his dusty breeches—"I don't care if a man is a blue Martian with two heads and four mouths—if he can keep those mouths shut and do his job! It's the job which counts here, and, according to Morgan, you have something useful to contribute. Make up your mind and let me know. If you don't want to play—we'll ship you out tonight, tell your brother that you're on government work, and keep you quiet for a while. Sorry, but that's the way it will have to be."

Travis smiled at that promise. He thought he could get out of here safely on his own if he really wanted to. But now he prodded the Major a little.

"Expedition back to catch a Folsom man—" But Kelgarries might not have heard, for he had already turned away. Travis followed, to come upon Ashe.

The latter was engaged in assembling a tripod of slender rods with the care of one handling brittle and precious objects. He glanced up as Travis' shadow fell across his work.

"Decided to join us for a look-see into the past?"

"Do you really mean you *can* do that?"

"We've done more than look." Ashe adjusted a screw delicately. "We've been there."

Travis stared. He could accept the fact of a new and greatly improved Vis-Tex to provide a peephole

27

into history and prehistory. But time travel was something else.

"It's perfectly true," Ashe finished with the screw. His attention passed from the tripod to Travis. And there was that in his manner which carried conviction.

"And we're going back again."

"After a Folsom man?" demanded the Apache incredulously.

"After a spaceship."

3

THIS was no dream, not even a very realistic one. There was Ashe, his fingers busy, his brown face outlined against the red and yellow walls of the cliff and the crumbling ruins they enclosed. This was here and now—yet what Ashe was saying, soberly, and in detail, was the wildest fantasy.

". . . so we discovered the Reds had time travel and were prospecting back into the past. What they dredged up there couldn't be explained by any logic based on the history we knew and the prehistory we had pieced out. What we didn't know then was that they had found the remains—badly smashed—of a spaceship. It was encased in the ice of Siberia, along with preserved mammoth bodies and a few other pertinent clues to suggest the proper era for them to explore. They muddied the trail as well as they could be establishing way stations in other periods of time. Then we chanced on one of those middle points. And the Reds themselves by capturing our time agents, showed us the ship they were plundering some thousands of years earlier.''

The story made sense—in a crazy kind of way. Travis mechanically handed Ashe the small tool he was groping for in the tangled grass.

"But how did the ship get there?" he asked. "Was there an early civilization on earth which had space travel?"

"That was what we thought—until we found the ship. No, it was from the outside—a cargo freighter lost from some galactic run. Either this world was an astrogation menace of the same type as a reef at sea, or there was some other reason to cause forced landings here. We brought film from the Red time station pinpointing about a dozen such wrecks. And some of those were on this side of the Atlantic.''

"You're planning to dig for one of those *here?*"

Ashe laughed. "What d'you think we'd find after about fifteen thousand years and a lot of land upheaval, even local volcanic activity? We want our ship in as good condition as possible.''

"To study?"

"With caution. If you'd check with Ross Murdock he'd give you a good reason for the caution. He was one of our agents who was actually aboard the ship the Reds were plundering. When they cornered him in the control cabin, he accidentally activated the com system and called in the real owners. They weren't too pleased with the Reds—came down and destroyed their time base on that level and then followed them through the other way stations, destroying each. Remember that hush-hush bang in the Baltic early this year? That was the 'space patrol,' or whatever they call themselves, putting finis to the Red project. So far as we know they didn't discover that we were and are interested in the same thing. So if we find our ship here, we walk softly along its corridors."

"You want the cargo?"

"In part. But mostly we want the knowledge—what its designers had—the key to space."

The thrill of that touched Travis. Mankind had reached for the stars for almost two generations. Men had had small successes, many searing failures. Now—what was a satisfactory flight to the barren moon compared to star flight and what lay far out?

Ashe, reading his expression, smiled. "You feel it too, don't you?"

The Apache nodded absently, gazing down the canyon, trying to believe that somewhere about here, trapped in the solid wall of time, there lay a wrecked star ship waiting for them. But he could not even visualize this country as it must have been in pluvial times. When rain fell most of the year, it must have made a morass of the lands outside the encroaching arms of the shrinking glaciers lying not too far northward.

"But why the Folsom points?" Out of the welter of facts and half facts he picked that as a starting point.

"We've sent back agents disguised as pre-Celts, as Tartars—or their remoter ancestors—as Bronze

Age Beaker Traders, and in half a hundred other character parts. Now there's a chance we may have to produce a few Folsom spearmen. One of the first and most important rules of this game, Fox, is that one does not interfere with time by introducing any modernisms. There must be no hint of our agents' real identity. We have no idea what might happen if one meddled with the stream of history as we know it, and we trust we'll never have to find out the hard way.''

''Hunters,'' Travis said slowly, hardly aware at that moment that he spoke at all. ''Mammoth—mastodon—camels—the dire wolf—sabertooth—''

''Why do all those interest you?''

''Why?'' Travis echoed and then stopped to examine his reasons. Why *had* his reaction to Ashe's picture of the drifting prehistoric hunters in disguise been his own quick inner vision of a land peopled with strange beasts his own race had never hunted? Or had they? Had the Folsom hunters been his remote ancestors, as the pre-Celt and Beaker Trader Ashe mentioned been the other's fore-fathers? He only knew that he had experienced a sudden thrust of excitement which lingered with him. There built up in him a desire to see that world which his own age knew only by the dim and often contradictory evidence of rocks, a handful of flint points, broken bones, the ancient smears of vanished cooking fires.

''My people were hunters—long after yours followed another way of life,'' he said, making the best answer he could.

''Right.'' Ashe's tone held a note of satisfaction. ''Now—just reach me that rod.'' He went back to

the job at hand and Travis settled down as his somewhat bewildered assistant. The Apache knew that he
had made the choice Kelgarries wanted—that he was
going to be a part of this whole unbelievable adventure.

The one thing he was sure of during the next two
crowded days was that they were indeed working
under pressure and against time. Whether the un-
explained threat which seemed to overhang the
whole project came from outside the country or from
fear of a policy change here at home, no one
bothered to make clear. But Travis was willing not to
inquire about that. It was far more interesting and
absorbing to work with Ross Murdock. They set the
proper kind of shafts to the pseudo-Folsom spear
points and then experimented with the spear
thrower. This made the efficient weapons they finally turned out twice as powerful. A seven-foot
javelin could be hurled a good hundred and fifty
yards or more by the use of that two-foot shaft of the
thrower, and Travis knew that in close infighting it
would add tremendous thrusting power. No wonder
a party of hunters so armed dared to go against the
mammoth and the other giant mammals of the
period.

In addition to the spears they had flint knives, the
counterparts of those found in the debris of Folsom
camp sites across most of western America. Travis
did not know why he was so sure that he was actually
going to use knife and spears and play the role of a
wandering prehistoric hunter. Still, he was sure. He
learned from Ross that the rest of the time agents'
equipment would not be assembled at the base until

the experts had taped film reports out of the past to use as samples.

On the third day Kelgarries and Ashe took a three-man expedition, loading one 'copter to its limit, out of the canyon. They were gone for almost a week, and upon their return some reels of film were sent out in a hurry. Ashe joined Travis and Ross that same night and lay down beside the fire with a sigh of weary pleasure.

"Hit pay dirt?" Ross wanted to know.

His chief nodded. There were dark smudges under his eyes, a fine, drawn look to his features. "The wreck is there, all right. And we located hunters on the fringe of the territory. But I think we can follow Plan One. The tribe is small and there doesn't appear to be more than one. Our guess that the district was thinly populated must be correct. It won't be necessary to really establish our scouts with the tribe—just let them keep track of wandering hunters."

"And the transfer?"

Ashe glanced at the watch on his wrist. "Harvey and Logwood are assembling the new one. I give them about forty-eight hours. H.Q. will fly in the extra power packs tonight. Then our men go through. We haven't the time to spend on finer points now. A working crew follows as soon as the scouts give the 'all clear.' H.Q. is analyzing the film reports. They'll have the rest of the equipment to us as soon as possible."

Travis stirred. Who was going to be part of that scouting team into the far past? He wanted to ask that—to hope that he might be one. But what had happened a year ago to smash other plans, kept him tongued-tied now. Ross voiced that all-important question.

"Who makes the first jump, chief?"

"You—me—we're on the spot. Our friend here, if he wants to."

"You mean that?" Travis asked slowly.

Ashe reached for the waiting coffeepot. "Fox, as long as you don't go loping off on your own to test that flint-tipped armory you've been constructing on the first available mammoth, you can come along. Mainly because you look the part, or will when we get through with you. And maybe you can adapt better than we can. Briefing for a time run used to take weeks. Ask Ross here; he can tell you what a cram course in our work is like. But today we haven't weeks to spare. We've only days and they grow fewer with each sunrise. So we're gambling on you, on Ross, on me. But get this—I'm your section leader, the orders come from me. And the main rule is—the job comes first! We keep away from the natives, we don't get involved in any happenings back there. Our only reason for going through is to make as sure as we can that the technical boys are not going to be distrubed while they work on that wreck. And that may not be an easy job."

"Why?" Ross asked.

"Because this ship didn't make as good a landing as the one you saw the Reds stripping. According to the films we took through the peeper there was a bad smash when it hit dirt. We may have to let it go altogether and track down Number Two on our list. Only, if we *can* come up with just one good find on board this one, we can stave off the objections of the

Committee and get the appropriation for future exploration.''

''Might do to run one of the Committee through,'' Ross remarked.

Ashe grinned. ''Want to lose your job, boy? Give 'em a good look around in some of the spots we've prospected and they'd turn up their toes—quick.''

Just three days later a bright shaft of sunlight illuminated a small side pocket of the canyon spotlighting the three as they worked. They were under the highly critical eyes of a small, neat man who regarded them intently through the upper half of his bifocals and made terse suggestions in a dry, precise voice. Stripping, they rubbed into their skins inch by inch the cream their instructor had provided. And under that oiling their tanned, or naturally dark, skins took on the leathery, uniform browness of men who wore very little clothing in any kind of weather.

Ashe and Ross had been provided with contact lenses so that their eyes were now as dark brown as Travis'. And their closely cropped hair was hidden under finely made wigs of straggling, coarse black locks which fell shoulder-length at the sides and descended as a pony's mane between their shoulder blades.

Then each took his turn flat on his back while the make-up artist, working from film charts, proceeded to supply his victims with elaborate patterns of simulated tatoos, marking chests, upper arms, chins, and upper cheekbones. Travis, undergoing the process, studied Ashe, who now represented the finished product. Had he not seen all the steps in that transformation, he would not have guessed that under that savage shell now existed Dr. Gordon Ashe.

"Glad we're allowed sandals," the same savage commented as he tightened the thongs which held about him a combination lioncloth-kilt of crudely dressed hide.

Ross had just thrust his bare feet into a pair of such primitive footwear. "Let's hope they'll stay on if we have to scramble, chief," he said, eying them dubiously.

Finished at last, the three stood in line to be checked by the make-up man and Kelgarries. The Major carried some furred skins over his arm, and now he tossed one to each of the disguised men.

"Better hold on to those. It gets cold where you're going. All right—the 'copter's waiting."

Travis slung a hide pouch over his shoulder and gathered up the three spears he had headed with pseudo-Folsom points. All the men were armed with the same weapons and there was a supply bag for each man.

The 'copter took them up and out, swinging away from the Canyon of the Hohokam into a wide sweep of desert land, bringing them down again before a carefully camouflaged installation. Kelgarries gave Ashe his last instructions.

"Take a day—two if you have to. Make a circle about five miles out, if you can. The rest is up to you."

Ashe nodded. "Can do. We'll signal in as soon as we can give an 'all clear.' "

The concealed structure housed a pile of material

and an inner erection of four walls, one floor, no roof. Together the three agents crowded into that, watched the panel slide to behind them, while a radiance streamed up around their bodies. Travis felt a tingling through bone and muscle, and then a stab which was half panic as the breath was squeezed from his lungs by a weird wrenching that twisted his insides. But he kept his feet, held on to his spears. There was a second or two of blackness. Then once again he gulped air, shook himself as he might have done climbing out of strong river current. Ross's dot-bordered lips curved in a smile and he signaled "thumbs up" with his scarred hand.

"End of run—here we go. . . ."

As far as Travis could see they were still in the box. But when Ashe pushed open the door panel, they looked out not on the piled boxes which had lain there before but upon an untidy heap of rocks. And clambering over those in the wake of his companions, the Apache did find a very different world before him.

Gone was the desert with its burden of sun-heated rock. A plain of coarse grass, thigh-, even waist-high, rolled away to some hills. And that grassy plain was cut by the end of a lake which stretched northward beyond the horizon. Travis saw brush and small trees dotting in clumps. And, too distant for him to distinguish their species, he could make out slowly moving lumps which could only be grazing animals.

There was a sun overhead, but a cold, harassing wind whipped with an ice-tipped lash around Travis' three-quarters-bare body. He pulled the hide robe about his shoulders, and saw that his companions had copied that move. The air was not only chilly, it was dank with a wealth of moisture. And there were new, rank smells, which his nostrils could not identify, carried by each puff of breeze. This world was as harsh and grim as his own, but in a very different fashion.

Ashe stooped and rolled aside one of the nearby rocks to disclose a small box. From his supply bag he produced three small buttons, giving one to each of the younger men.

"Plant that in your left ear," he ordered, and did so with his own. Then he pushed a key on the side of the box. Instantly a low chirruping sound was audible. "This is our homing signal. It acts as radar to bring you back here."

"What's that?"

A plume of smoke, whipped by the wind into a long trail of gray-white vapor, bannered to the north. From the shape Travis could not believe that it marked a forest fire, yet it surely signalized a conflagration of some size.

Ashe glanced up casually. "Volcano," he returned. "This part of the world hasn't settled down too stably yet. We head northwest, around the lake tip, and we should strike the wreck." He started off at a steady lope which told Travis that this was not the first time the time agent had played the role of primitive hunter.

The grass brushed against them, leaving drops of cold moisture on their bare legs and thighs. Travis concluded that there must have been rain very shortly before their arrival. And from the look of the massing clouds to the east, a second storm might catch them soon.

As they came away from the hill whose foot sheltered the time transfer, that chirruping in his ear grew fainter, varying in intensity as Ashe twisted and turned about the hooked end of the lake. The wide reach of lush grass continued and this was truly game country. As yet, though they had not passed close enough to any of the grazers to see what type of animals they were.

About a half mile from the curving shore of the lake rested an object which was not natural. Pushed deep into the earth, its rounded side showing two jagged rents, lay a half globe of metallic material Around it was a wide patch of blackened earth only raggedly striped with new grass. But what impressed Travis chiefly was the object's size. He deduced that perhaps only half of the thing was visible—if its form had originally been a true globe. Yet that half now above the earth was at least six stories tall. The complete vessel must have been a vertible monster, more equal to an ocean liner than the largest sky transport he knew of in his own time.

"She certainly got it!" observed Ross. "Bad crack up at landing—"

"Or else she had it before landing." Ashe leaned on a spear to survey the hulk.

"What—?"

"Those holes might have been caused by shell fire. We'll leave that to the experts to determine. But this could be a wreck from a space battle. That storm's coming fast. I say we'd better circle west ahead of it and find some shelter in the hills. If the first reports are correct, we'll be caught in a kind of rain we know nothing about!''

Ashe's lope lengthened into a trot, and the trot into a space-covering run. He was heading away from the wrecked ship to the distant hills, and to reach them they had to round the narrow end of the lake.

They were carefully threading their way through the edge of a marshy spot when a scream halted them. Travis knew that it was a death cry, but the sound was followed by an appalling, yowling squall which could come from no throat, animal or human, of his own time. It sounded from directly before them. The squall was answered in turn by a grunting, such a grunting as might have issued from the deep chest of a giant pig. And that grunting was echoed on a higher note almost directly behind them!

"Down!" Travis obeyed the order from Ashe, throwing himself flat on the muddy ground, wriggling to the left. A moment later all three scouts huddled in a growth of tough brush. They paid no attention to the torment inflicted by its brambles on their arms and shoulders, for they had front-row seats on a wild drama which held them enthralled.

Crumpled on the ground was a mound of heaving flesh, plainly in the death throes, its long, shaggy yellow hair sodden with blood. Crouched at bay behind that body was another animal. Travis could classify it when he caught sight of those long, curved fangs: sabertooth. It was slightly shorter than a lion of Travis' own day, and its muscular legs and powerful shoulders displayed a threat of force which would daunt a larger beast. But now it was facing a giant. . . .

The opponent, whose cub had been killed, was a mountain of flesh, rearing almost eighteen feet above the ground. Balanced on large-boned hind feet and thick tail, it fronted the sabertooth with powerful forearms, each tipped with a gigantic single claw. The narrow head twisted and turned above the slender forebody, the thick brown hair covering it in constant movement.

There was a rank smell of animal blown to the men in the brush as a second monstrous ground sloth moved in to give battle. And the sabertooth spat like the enraged cat it was.

4

A HAND closed on Travis' arm, jerking his attention from the shaping battle. Ashe pointed westward and pulled again. Ross was already creeping in that direction. The wind was at their back so that they caught the fetor of the beasts without danger of their being scented in turn.

"Get to it!" Ashe ordered. "We don't want that cat on our trail. It can't take on two adult sloths and it'll be one mighty disappointed diner—out looking for another meal pretty soon now."

They wormed their way forward, trying to gauge from the squalls of the cat, the grunting of the sloths, whether battle had yet reached the stage of actual blows. If the cat was smart, Travis knew, it would let itself be driven off. And knowing the tactics of mountain lions of *his* southwest, he believed that that was what would happen.

"Okay—run!" Ashe scrambled to his feet and set a good pace across the open lands, the other two thudding behind him. The sun had completely disappeared now, and the grayness under those lowering clouds approached twilight. The thin chirrup of their homing device sounded very lonely and far away.

Brown-gray lumps swung up heads with wide stretches of horns. Save that those horns were straight and not curved, the animals might have been the bison of the historic plains. Catching the scent of the scouts, they tossed those horned heads, set off northward down the open land at a lumbering gallop. Among them ran with speed and far more grace large-headed horses equipped with the spectacularly striped coats of zebras. This was plainly a hunter's paradise.

The rain came from behind the men, making a visible curtain of water. When that enfolded them, Travis gasped, choked, fought for breath under the flood which beat and pounded him. But his legs kept the striding pace Ashe had set, and the three continued to head for the hills which were now only vaguely visible through the downpour.

A rising slope slowed them, and twice they had to leap runnels of streams carrying away the excess of water being dumped on the heights above them. Lightning cracked with a lashing viciousness, bringing a scrap of illumination with it. A hand caught at Travis to the left, and so into partial shelter from the storm.

He was crowded together with Ashe and Ross, half crouching in the lee of some rocks. It was not quite a cave, but the crevice was better than the open slope.

"How long will this last?" Ross growled.

Ashe returned without much hope, "Anywhere from an hour to a couple of days. Let's hope we're lucky."

They squatted, drawing their hide robes about them, pressing together for the warmth of body contact in the midst of that damp cold. Perhaps they dozed, for Travis became aware of his surroundings with a jerk of his head which hurt neck and shoulder. He knew that the rain *had* stopped, though there was night outside their inadequate shelter. He asked:

"Do we move on?"

But the reply to that came from the world outside their hiding place, with a roar loud enough to split eardrums. Travis, his nails digging into the wooden shaft of his spear, could not control the shudder which shook him at that menacing blast.

"We do if we want to provide a midnight snack for our friend out there," Ashe commented. "The rain probably spoiled hunting for somebody. Hereabouts we have sabertooth, the Alaskan lion, the cave bear, and a few other assorted carnivores I don't want to meet without, say, a tank in reserve support."

"Cheery spot," Ross remarked. "I'd say our playmate upridge hasn't had much luck tonight. Any chance of his coming down to scoop us out—or try for taste?"

"If he, she or it does, he'll get a pawful of spear points." Ashe replied. "One advantage of this hole, nothing can get in if we're firm in saying No!"

There was a second roar, from farther away, Travis noted with relief. Whatever meat hunter on the hoof prowled the hills, it would not have followed their trail. The rain must have cleansed their scent from grass and earth. But they continued to huddle there, stiff and cold, endeavoring now and then to change position of arms or legs so that morning would not find them too cramped to move. They remained until the sky did lighten with the first sign of dawn.

Travis crawled out, straightened up painfully, and bit back a stinging word or two, as a morning breeze with the crispness of about three below zero cut in under the flap of his cloak blanket. He decided that to be properly prepared to roam the Pleistocene world in the garb of its rightful inhabitants, one should practice beforehand by spending a month or so in a deep freeze stripped to one's shorts. And he was pleased to see that neither Ashe nor Ross was any more agile when he emerged from the hole of refuge.

They mouthed food-concentrate tablets from their storage bags. Travis, though knowing the energy-building uses of those small pellets, longed for real meat, hot, yet still juicy, taken straight from the searing of the fire. There was no taste to these pill things.

"Up we go." Ashe wiped the back of his hand across his mouth and slung his bag over his shoulder. He studied the way before them to pick out the best ascent. But Travis had already started, winding in and out between boulders which marked the debris of a landslide.

When the scouts at last reached the summit, they

turned to look back into the valley of the lake. That smooth sheet of water occupied perhaps half of the basin. And it seemed to Travis that the mirror surface reached closer to the wrecked ship today than it had when they passed it the afternoon before. He said as much, and Ashe agreed.

"Water has to go somewhere and these rains feed all the streams heading down there. Another reason why we must make this a fast job. So—let's get moving."

But when they turned again to follow the line of the heights, Travis halted. A very thin and watery sunlight broke through the clouds, carrying with it little or no warmth as yet, but providing more light. And—he peered intently westward and downslope on the other side of the hills. . . . No, he had not been mistaken! That sunlight, feeble as it was, reflected from some point in the second valley. From water? He doubted that, the answering spark was too brilliant.

Ashe and Ross, following his direction, saw it too.

"Second ship?" Ross suggested.

"If so, it is not marked on our charts. But we'll take a look. I agree that's too bright to be sun on water."

Had there been survivors from the other crash? Travis wondered. If so, had they established a camp down there? He had heard enough during the past few days to judge that any contact with the original owners of the galactic ships could be highly dangerous. Ross had been pursued by one of their patrols across miles of wilderness, and had escaped from a form of mind compulsion they exerted only by delib-erately burning his hand in a fire and using pain to counter their mental demand for surrender. They were not human, those ship people, and what powers or weapons they did possess were so alien as to defy Terran understanding so far.

So the three took to cover, making expert use of every bit of brush, every boulder, as they advanced to locate that source of reflection. Again Travis was amazed by the skill of his companions. He had hunted lion, and lion in the beast's native mountains is very wary game. And he could read trail with all the skill imparted to him by Chato who knew the ways of the old raiding warriors. But these two were equal to him at what he always considered a red man's rather than a white man's game.

They came at last to lie in a fringe of trees, parting the grass cautiously to look out on an expanse of open land. In the middle of it rested another globe ship. But this one was entirely above ground and it was small, a pygmy compared to the giant in the other valley. At first superficial examination it looked to have been landed normally, not crashed. Halfway up, the curve facing them showed the dark hole of an open entrance port, and from it dangled a ladder. Someone *had* survived this landing, come to earth here!

"Lifeboat?" Ashe's voice was the slightest of whispers.

"It is not shaped like the one I saw before," Ross hissed. "That was like a rocket."

Wind sang across the clearing. Under its push the ladder clanged against the side of the globe. And from the foot of the strange ship some birds tried to rise. But they moved sluggishly, flopping their wings with an awkward heaviness. And the wind brought to the three in hiding that sweetish, stomach-turning odor which could never be mistaken by those who had ever smelled it. Something lay dead there, very dead.

Ashe stood up, watching those birds narrowly. Then he walked forward. A snarl came from close to ground level. Travis' spear came up. It sang through the air and a browncoated, four-footed beast yelped, leaped pawing in the air, to crash back into the grass. More of the gorged carrion birds fluttered and hopped away from their feast.

What lay about the foot of the ladder was not a pretty sight. Nor could the scouts tell at first glance how many bodies there had been. Ashe attempted to make a closer examination and came away, white-faced and gagging. Ross picked up a tatter of blue-green material.

"Baldies' uniforms, all right," he identified it. "This is one thing I'll never forget. What happened here? A fight?"

"What ever it was, it happened some time ago," Ashe, livid under tan and skin stain, got out the words carefully. "Since there was no burial, I'd say the crew must all have been finished."

"Do we go in?" Travis laid a hand on the ladder.

"Yes. But don't touch anything. Especially any of the instruments or installations."

Ross laughed on a slightly hysterical high note. "That you do not need to underline for me, chief. After you, sir, after you."

Thus, Ashe leading the way, they climbed the ladder, entered the gaping hole of the port. There was a second door a short distance inside, doubly thick and with heavy braces, but it, too, was ajar. Ashe pushed it back and then they were in a well from which another ladder-like stair arose.

Somehow Travis had expected darkness, since there were no windows or wall outlets in the outer skin of the globe. But a blue light seeped from the walls about them, and not only light, but a warmth which was comforting.

"The ship's still alive," Ross commented. "And if she *is* intact—"

"Then," Ashe finished softly for him, "we've made the *big* find, boys. We never hoped for luck like this." He started to climb the inner ladder.

They came to a landing, or rather a platform from which opened three oval doors, all closed. Ross pushed against each, but they all held.

"Locked?" Travis asked.

"Might be—or else we don't know how to turn the right buttons. Going on up, chief? If this follows the pattern of that other one, the control cabin is on top."

"We'll take a look. But no experiments, remember?"

Ross stroked his scarred hand. "I'm not forgetting that."

A second ladder section brought them through a manhole in the floor of a hemisphere chamber occupying the whole top of the ship. And, before they were through that entrance, they knew that death had come that way before them.

There was one body only, crumpled forward against the straps of a seat which hung on springs and cords from the roof. In front of that rigid corpse, which was clad in the blue-green material, was a board crowded with dials, buttons, levers.

"Pilot—died at his post." Ashe walked forward, stooped over the body. "I don't see any sign of a wound. Could be an epidemic which attached all the crew. We'll let the doctors figure it out."

They did not linger to explore farther, for this find was too important. It was too necessary that the news of this second ship be relayed to Kelgarries and his superiors. But Ashe took the precaution of drawing the ladder into the globe's port after his two younger companions had descended. He made his way down by rope.

"Who do you think is going to snoop?" Ross wanted to know.

"Just a little insurance. We know there are primitives in the northern end of this country. They may be the type to whom everything strange is taboo. Or they may be inquisitive enough to explore. And I don't fancy someone touching off a com again and calling in the galactic patrol or whoever those chaps wearing blue are. Now, let's get to the transfer on the double!"

The weak sunlight of the early morning had increased in strength. The air was growing noticeably warmer, and danker, too, as the moisture-laden grass about them gave up its burden of last night's rain. The process of travel resembled running through a river choked with slimy, slapping reeds, save that the ground underfoot was firm. The men panted up the heights, down past their refuge of the stormy night, to the plain of the lake, skirting the glade where scavengers were busy with the remains of the sabertooth's kill.

As they came out into the open Ashe broke stride and swept one hand down in an emphatic order to take cover. That herd of mixed bison and horses which they had startled the night before was in movement once more, cutting diagonally across their path. And the animals were plainly in flight from some menace. Sabertooth again? The bison, though, tons of heavy bone and meat not to be faced down with ease, appeared able to take care of themselves with those sweeping horns.

Only when the wind bore to Travis those high, far-off sounds which his ears translated into shouts from what must be human throats, did he understand that the hunters were out in force. The primitive tribesmen had in some manner stampeded the herd in order to cut down the weaker stragglers.

The scouts were pinned down, as an ever-thickening stream of animals cut across the road they must take in order to reach the time transport. Before they had reached their present position, the main body of the herd had caught up, headed by the fleeter horses which whirled ahead of the heavier bison in skimming flight. Now the men caught sight of other harriers, using the general disturbance to their own advantage. Five dark shapes broke cover a hundred yards or so away, weaving in to cut around a lumbering, half-grown calf on the edge of the running bison herd.

"Dire wolves," Ashe identified.

They were stocky, large-headed animals, running without giving tongue, but with a workmanlike weaving which displayed their familiarity with this game. Two darted in to snap at the calf's head, while the others rushed to try to deliver that crippling tendon slash of the hind legs which would make the bison easy prey.

"Oooooo-yahhh!"

That small drama so near to them had absorbed Travis almost to the point of his forgetting what must lie beyond. There was no chance yet of sighting those who called and made the stragglers their targets. But at that moment a horse staggered on past the bison which was fighting off the attentions of the wolves. Its large head had sunk close to knee level and a rope of bloody foam hung from muzzle to trampled grass. Driven deeply into its barrel was a spear. And even as the animal came fully into sight it tried to lift its head, faltered, and crashed to earth.

One of the wolves straightway turned attention to this new prey. It trotted away from the battle with the calf to sniff inquiringly at the still-breathing horse and then, with a growl, to launch itself at the animal's throat. The wolf was feeding when the hunter of that kill made a swift answer to such brazen theft.

Another spear, lighter, but as deadly and well aimed, sped through the air, caught the dire wolf behind the right shoulder. The wolf gave a convulsive leap and collapsed just beyond the body of the horse. At the same time other spears flashed, bringing down its pack mates and, last of all, the young bison they had been worrying.

Most of the fleeing herd had passed by now. There

were other animals lying on the flattened grass of the back trail. The three scouts crouched low, unable to withdraw lest they attract the notice of the hunters now coming in to collect their booty.

There were twenty or more males, medium-sized brown-skinned men with ragged heads of black hair like the wigs provided the scouts. Their clothing consisted of the same hide lioncloth-kilts fastened about their sweating bodies with string belts and lacings of thongs. Travis, studying them, could see how well their own make-up matched the general appearance of the Folsom hunters.

Behind the men trudged the women and children, stopping to butcher the kill. And there were more of these than of the hunters. Whether those they saw represented the full strength of a small tribe, there was no telling. The men shouted to each other hoarsely, and the two who had accounted for the wolves seemed especially pleased. One of them squatted on his heels, pried open the mouth of the wolf which had killed the horse, and inspected its fangs with a critical eye. Since a necklace of just such trophies strung on a thong thumped across his broad chest with every movement of his body, it was plain he was considering a new addition to his adornment.

Ashe's hand fell on Travis' shoulder. "Back," he breathed into the Apache's ear. They retreated, wriggling out of the grass into the edge of the morass at the end of the lake. Here with the muck covering their bodies, and flies and other stinging insects greeting them with avid appetites, they made their way on. They moved away from the scene of the hunt with every bit of stalker's skill they possessed, glad there was a wealth of meat to occupy the tribesmen.

Clumps of willow-like trees began to offer better screening, and behind these they achieved a hunched run until Ashe subsided, panting, into a convenient pile of brush. Travis, his chest an arch of hot pain which cut with every stabbing breath, threw himself face down, and Ross collapsed between the two.

"That was nearly it," Ross got out between rasping intakes of air. "Never a dull moment in this business. . . ."

Travis raised his head from his bent arm and tried to locate landmarks. They had been headed for the rockmasked time transport when the hunt cut across their path. But they had had to swing north to avoid the butchering parties. So their goal must now lie southeast.

Ashe was on his knees, peering northward to where the bulk of wrecked ship was embedded in the plain.

"Look!"

They drew up beside him to watch a party of the hunters patter around the wreckage. One of them raised a spear and clanged it against the side of the spaceship.

"They didn't avoid it." Travis got the significance of the casual assault.

"Which means—we'll have to move fast with the smaller one! If they discover it, they may try to explore. Time's growing shorter."

"Only open country between us and the transfer now." Travis pointed out the obvious. To cut directly across to that distant cluster of masking rocks would put them in the open, to be instantly sighted by any tribesman looking in the right direction.

Ashe gazed at him thoughtfully. "Do you think you could make it without being spotted?"

Travis measured distances, tried to pick out any scrap of cover lying along the shortest route. "I can try," was all he could say in return.

5

HE MADE for the rise at the southern point of which stood the pile of rocks masking the installation. A brindled shape slunk out of his path, showing fangs. Then the dire wolf trotted on to the nearest carcass, where the women had stripped only the choicest meat, to investigate food for which it would not have to fight.

Travis worked his way along the foot of the rise. The main path of the stampede was to the west and he believed himself in the clear, when there was a snorting before him. A bulk heaved through small bushes and he found himself fronting a bison cow. Too high on her shoulder to cause a disabling wound, a broken spear shaft protruded. And the pain had enraged her to a dangerous state.

In such a situation even a range cow would be

perilous for a man on foot, and the bison was a third again as big as the animals he knew. Only the bushes around them saved Travis from death at that first meeting. The cow bellowed and charged, bearing down on him at a speed which he would have believed impossible for her weight. He hurled himself to the left in a wild scramble to escape and found himself in a thorny tangle. The cow, meanwhile, burst past him close enough for the coarse mat of her hair to rasp against one outflung arm.

Travis' head rang with the sound of her bellowing as he squirmed around in the bush to bring up his heaviest spear. The cow had skidded to a stop, tearing up matted grass and turf with her hoofs as she wheeled. Then the spear haft in her shoulder caught in one of the springy half-trees. She bellowed again, lurching forward to fight that drag until the broken spear ripped loose and a great gout of blood broke, to be sopped up in the heavy tangle of shoulder hair.

That slowed her. Travis had time to get on his feet, ready his spear. There was no good target in that wide head confronting him. He jerked off his supply bag, swung it by its carrying thong, and flung it at the cow's dripping muzzle. His trick worked. The bison charged, not for him, but after the thing which had teased her. And Travis thrust home behind the shoulder with all the force he had.

The weight of the bison and the impetus of the animal's charge tore the shaft from his hold. Then the cow went to her knees, coughing, and the big body rolled on one side. He hurdled the mount of her hindquarters, fearing that the noise of battle might attract the hunters.

Forcing a way through the brush, he made most of the remainder of his journey on hands and knees. At last he crouched in the shelter of the rock pile, his ribs heaving, careless of the bleeding scratches which laced his arms and shoulders, stung on cheek and chin.

Watching his back trail, his body pressed to earth, Travis saw that he had been wise to leave the scene of battle quickly. Three of the hunters were running across the plain toward the brush, trailing spears. But they went with caution enough to suggest that this was not the first time they had had to deal with wounded stragglers from a stampeded herd.

Having scouted the bush, the brown men ventured into its cover. And seconds later a surprised shout informed Travis his kill had been located. Then that shout was answered by a long eerie wail from some point up the hill above the rocks. Travis stirred uneasily.

The spear he had been forced to leave in the body of the cow resembled their own—but did it look enough like theirs for them to believe the kill had been made by a tribesman? Had these people some system of individual markings for personal weapons, such as his own race had developed in their roving days? Would they try to track him down?

He snaked his way into the crevice of the rocks. The alerting signal was there, a second box set in beside the radar guide which now hummed its signal in his ear. He plunged down the lever set in its lid, then moved the tiny bit of metal rapidly up and down in the pattern he had been drilled in using only the day before. In the desert of the late twentieth century that call would register on another recording device, relaying to Kilgarries the need for a hasty conference.

Travis edged out from the rocks and looked about him warily. He flattened against a boulder taller than his wiry body and listened, not only with his ears but with every wilderness-trained sense he possessed. His flint knife was in his fist as he caught that click of warning. And his other hand went out to grab at an upraised forearm as brown and well muscled as his own. The smell of blood and grease hit his nostrils as they came together breast to breast, and the stranger spat a torrent of unintelligible words at him. Travis brought up the fist with the knife, not to strike into the other's flesh, but in a sharp blow against a thick jawbone. It was a blow that rocked the round black head back on the slightly hunched shoulders.

Pain scored along his own ribs as the two men broke apart. He aimed another blow at the jaw, brought up his knee as the native sprang in, knife ready. It was dirty fighting according to the rules of civilization, but Travis wanted a quick knockout with no knife work. He staggered the hunter, and was going in for a last telling blow when another figure darted around the rocks and struck at the back of the tribesman's head, sending him limp and unconscious to the ground.

Ross Murdock wasted no time in explanations. "Come on. Help me get him under cover!"

Somehow they crowded into the shelter of the transfer, the Folsom man between them. And Ross, with quick efficiency, tied the wrists and ankles of their captive and inserted a strip of hide for a gag between his slack jaws.

Travis inspected a dripping cut across his own ribs, decided it was relatively unimportant, and then faced about as Ashe joined them.

"Looks as if you've been elected target for today." Ashe pushed aside Travis' hands to inspect the cut critically. "You'll live," he added, as he rummaged in his supply bag for a small box of pills. One he crushed on his palm, to smear the resulting powder along the bloody scratch, the other he ordered his patient to swallow. "What did you do to touch this off?"

Travis sketched his adventure with the bison cow.

Ashe shrugged. "Just one of those unlucky foulups we have to expect now and then. Now we have this fellow to worry about." He surveyed the captive bleakly.

"What do we do?" Ross's nose wrinkled. "Start a zoo with this exhibit one?"

"You got the message through? Ashe asked.

Travis nodded.

"Then we'll sit it out. As soon as it gets dark we'll carry him out, cut the cords, and leave him near one of their camps. That's the best we can do. Unfortunately the tribe seems to be heading west—"

"West!" Travis thought of that other ship.

"What if they try to board that spacer?" Ross seemed to share his concern. "I've a feeling this isn't going to be a lucky run. We've had trouble breathing down our necks right from the start. But we should keep watch on that other ship—"

"And what *could* we do to prevent their exploring it?" Travis wanted to know. He was in a deflated mood, willing to agree with any forebodings.

"We'll hope that they will follow the herd," Ashe answered. "Food is a major preoccupation with such a tribe and they'll keep near to a good supply as long as they can. But it does make sense to watch the ship. I'll have to wait here to report to Kelgarries. Suppose you two take our friend here for his walk and then keep on going to that ridge between the valleys. Then you can let us know in time to keep our men under cover if the tribe drifts that way."

Ross sighed. "All right, chief. When do we start?"

"At dusk. No use courting trouble. There will be prowlers out there after nightfall."

"Prowlers!" Ross grinned without much humor. "That's a mild way of putting it. I don't intend to meet up with any eleven-foot lion in the dark!"

"Moon tonight," corrected Travis mildly, and settled himself for what rest he could get before they ventured to leave.

Not only the moon gave light that night. The dusky sky was riven by the distant sullen fire of the volcano—or volcanoes. Travis now believed that there was more than one burning mountain to the north. And there was a distinct metallic taste in the air, which Ashe ascribed to an active eruption miles away.

Somehow, between them they got their captive on his feet and marched him along. He seemed to be in a dazed state, slumping again to the ground while Travis went ahead to scout out a group about a fire.

The Folsom men—and women—were gorging on meat lightly seared by the flames of the fire. The odor of it reached Travis and filled him with an urge to dart into that company and seize a sizzling rib or two for himself. Concentrates might provide the scientific balance of energy and nourishment which his body needed, but they were no substitute, as far as his personal tastes were concerned, for the materials of the feast he was watching.

Fearing to linger lest his appetite overpower his caution, he flitted back to Ross and reported that there were no sentries out to spoil their simple plan. So they hauled their charge to the edge of the firelight, removed his bonds and gag, and gave him a light push. Then they took to their heels in a spurt of speed designed to carry them out of range.

If any natives did follow, they did not find the right trail, and the two made the ridge without any more bad luck.

"We're the stupid ones," Ross observed as they drew up the last incline and found a reasonably sheltered spot under an overhand. It was not quite a cave, but had only one open side to defend. "Nobody in his right senses is going to gallop around in the dark."

"Dark?" protested Travis, clasping his arms about the knees pulled tightly to his chest, and staring northward. His suspicions about the volcanic activity there was borne out now by the redness of the sky, the presence of fumes in the wind. It was a spectacular display, but one which did not give confidence to the viewer. His only satisfaction lay in the miles which must stretch between that angry mountain and the ridge on which he was now stationed.

Ross made no answer. Since Travis had the first watch, his companion had rolled in his hide cloak and was already asleep.

It was a broken night and when Travis arose in the dawn he discovered a thin skim of gray dust on his skin and the rocks about. At the same time a sulphuric blast in his face made him cough raggedly.

"Anything doing below?" he croaked.

Ross shook his head and offered the gourd water bottle. The small spaceship rested peacefully below and the only change in the picture from the day previous was that there was not so much activity among the scavengers below the open port.

"What are they like—those men from space?" Travis asked suddenly.

To his surprise Ross, whom he had come to regard as close to nerveless, shivered.

"Pure poison, fella, and don't you ever forget it! I saw two kinds—the baldies who wear the blue suits, and a furry-faced one with pointed ears. They may look like men—but they aren't. And believe me, anyone who tangles with those boys in blue is asking to be chopped up fine in a grinder!"

"I wonder where they came from." Travis raised his head. There were a few stars, still dim pinpoints of light in the dawn sky. To think of those as suns nourishing other worlds such as the solid earth now under him—where men, or at least creatures fashioned something like men, carried on lives of their own—was a spread of imagination requiring some effort of mind.

Ross waved a hand skyward. "Take your pick,

Fox. The big brains running this show of ours believe there was a whole confederation of different worlds tied together in a United Something-or-other then—'' He blinked and then laughed. ''Me— saying 'then' when I mean 'now!' This jumping back and forth in time mixes a guy's thinking.''

''And if someone were to take off in that ship down there, he'd run into them outside?''

''If he did, he'd regret it!''

''But if he took off in our time—would he still find them waiting?''

Ross played with the thongs fastening the supply bag. ''That's one of the big questions. And nobody'll have the right answer until we do go and see. Twelve—fifteen thousand years is a long time. Do you know any civilization here that's lasted even a fraction of that? From painted hunters to the atom here. Out there it could be the atom back to painted hunters—or to nothing—by now.''

''Would you like to go and see?''

Ross smiled. ''I've had one brush with the blue boys. If I could be sure they weren't still on some star map, I might say yes. I wouldn't care to meet them on their home ground—and I'm no trained space man. But the idea does eat into a fella . . . . Ha— company!''

There was movement down in the valley—to the north. But those objects issuing out of the trees at a leisurely and ponderous pace were not Folsom hunters. Ross whistled very softly between his teeth, watching that advance eagerly, and Travis shared his excitement.

The bison herd, the striped horses, the frustrated

sabertooth confronting the giant ground sloths, none had been as thrilling a sight as this. Even the elephant of their own time could generate a measure of awe in the human onlooker by the sheer majesty of its movement, its aura of strength and fearlessness. And these larger and earlier members of the same tribe produced an almost paralyzing sense of wonder in the two scouts. "Mammoths!"

Tall, thick-haired giants, their backbones sloping from the huge dome of the skull, the hump of shoulder, to the shorter hindquarters dwarfed tree and landscape as they moved. Three of them towered close to fourteen feet at the shoulder. They bore the weight of the tremendous curled tusks proudly, their trunks swaying in time to their unhurried steps. They were the most formidable living things Travis had ever seen. And, watching them, he could not believe that the hunters he had spied upon in the other valley had ever brought down such game with spears. Yet the evidence that they had, had been discovered over and over again—scattered bones with a flint point between the giant ribs or splitting a massive spine.

"One—two—three—" Ross was counting, half under his breath. "And a small one—"

"Calf," Travis identified. But even that baby was nothing to face without a modern shotgun to hand.

"Four—five—Family party?" Ross speculated.

"Maybe. Or do they travel in herds?"

"Ask the big brains. Ohhh—look at that tree go!"

The leader in the dignified parade set its massive head against a tree bole, gave a small push, and the tree crashed. With a squeal audible to the scouts, the mammoth calf hustled forward and started harvesting the leaves with a busy trunk, while its elders appeared to watch it with adult indulgence.

Ross pushed the wind-blown tails of wig hair out of his eyes. "We may have a problem here. What if they don't move on? I can't see a crew working down there with those tons of tusks skipping about in the background."

"If you want to haze 'em on," Travis observed, "don't let me stop you. I've drag-herded stubborn cows—but I'm not going down there and swing a rope at any of those rumps!"

"They might take a fancy to bump over the ship."

"So they might," agreed Travis. "And what could we do to stop 'em?"

But for the moment the mammoth family seemed content at their own end of the valley, which was at least a quarter of a mile from the ship. After an hour's watch Ross tightened the thongs of his sandals and gathered up his spears.

"I'll report in. Maybe those walking mountains will keep hunters away—"

"Or draw them here," corrected Travis pessimistically. "Think you can find your way back?"

Ross grinned. "This trail is getting to be a regular freeway. All we need is a traffic cop or two. Be seeing you. . . ." He disappeared from their perch with that swift and silent ability to vanish into the surrounding landscape which Travis still found unusual in a white man.

As Travis continued to lie there, chin supported on forearm, idly watching the mammoths, he tried again to figure out what made Ashe and Ross Murdock so different from the other members of their race he knew. Of course he had in a measure felt the same lack of selfconciousness with Dr. Morgan. To Prentiss Morgan a man's race and the color of his skin were nothing—a shared enthusiasm was all that really mattered. Morgan had cracked Travis Fox's shell and let him into a larger world. And then—like all soft and de-shelled creatures—he had been the more deeply hurt when that new world had turned hostile. He had then fled back into the old, leaving everything—even friendship behind.

Now he waited for the old smoldering flame of anger to bite. It was there, but dulled, as the night fire of the volcano was now only a lazy smoke plume under the rising sun. The desert over which he had ridden to find water a week ago was indeed time buried. What—?

The mammoths had moved, with the largest bull facing about. Trunk up, the beast shrilled a challenge that tore at Travis' ears. This was beyond the squall of the sabertooth, the grunting roar of a sloth prepared to do battle. It was the most frightening sound he had ever heard.

A second time the bull trumpeted. Sabertooth on the hunt? The Alaskan lion? What animal was large enough, or desperate enough, to stalk that walking mountain? Man?

But if there was a Folsom hunter in hiding, he did not linger. The bull paced along the edge of the wood and then butted over another tree, to tear loose leaved branches and crunch them greedily. The crisis was past.

An hour later a party guided by Ross climbed up to join him. Kelgarries, and four others, wearing dull-green and brown coveralls which faded into the general background, spread themselves on the ground to share the lookout.

"That's our baby!" The Major's face was alight with enthusiasm as he sighted the derelict. "What can you do about her, boys?"

But one of the crew focused glasses in another direction. "Hey—those things are mammoths!" he shouted. As one, his fellow turned to follow his directing finger.

"Sure," snapped the Major. "Look at the ship, Wilson. If she is intact, can we possibly swing a direct transfer?"

Reluctantly the other man abandoned the mammoth family for business. He studied the derelict through his lenses. "Some job. Biggest transfer we ever did was the sub frame—"

"I know that! But that was two years ago, and Crawford's experiments have proved that the grid can be expanded without losing power. If we can take this one straight through without any dismantling, we've put the schedule ahead maybe five years! And you know what that will mean."

"And who's going to go down there to set up a grid with those outsize elephants watching him? We have to have a clear field to work in and no interruptions. A lot of the material won't stand any rough handling."

"Yeah," echoed one of his subordinates. Again the lenses swung to the north. "Just how are you going to shoo the mammoths out?"

"Scout job, I suppose." That resigned comment came from Ashe as he joined the party. "Well I'm admitting right here and now that I have no ideas, bright or otherwise, on how to make a mammoth decide to take a long walk. But we're open for suggestions.''

They watched the browsing beasts in silence. Nobody volunteered any ideas. It appeared that this particular problem was not yet covered by any rule on or off the book.

6

"WHAT WE need is a mine field—like the one planted around H.Q.," Ross said at last.

"Mine field?" repeated the man Kelgarries had called Wilson. Then he said again. "Mine field!"

"Got something?" demanded the Major.

"Not a mine field," Wilson corrected. "We could fix it for those brutes to blow themselves up, all right; but they'd take the ship with them. However, a sonic barrier now—"

"Run it around the ship outside your work field—yes!" The Major was eager again. "Would it take long to get it in?"

"We'd have to bring a lot of equipment through. Say a day—maybe more. But it is the only thing I can think of now which might work."

"All right. You'll get all the material you need—
on the double!" promised Kelgarries.

Wilson chuckled. "Just like that, eh? No howls
about expense? Remember, I'm not going to sign
any orders I have to defend with my lifeblood about
two years from now before some half-baked investigating committee."

"If we pull this off," Kelgarries returned with
convincing force, "We'll never have to defend anything before anyone! Man—you get that ship
through intact and our whole project will have paid
for itself from the day it was nothing but a few
wishful sentences on the back of an old envelope.
This is it—the big pay-off!"

That was the beginning of a hectic period in
Travis' life which he was never able to sort out neatly
in his head afterward. With Ashe and Ross he pa-
trolled a wide area of hill and valley, keeping watch
upon the camps of the wandering hunters, marking
down the drifting herds of animals. For two days
men shuttled back and forth and then erected a second time transfer within the valley of the smaller
ship.

Wilson's sonic barrier—an invisible yet nerve-
shattering wall of high-frequency impulses—was in
place around the ship. And while its signals did not
affect human ears, the tension it produced did reach
any man who strayed into its influence. The mammoth family withdrew into the small woodland from
which they had come. The men working on the globe
did not know whether that retreat was the result of
the vibrations or not—but at least the beasts were
gone.

Meanwhile more sonic broadcasters were set up on every path in and out of the valley, sealing it from invasion. Kelgarries and his superiors were throwing every resource of the project into this one job.

About the ship arose a framework of bars as fast as the men could fit one to another. Travis, watching the careful deliberation of the fitting, understood that delicate and demanding work was in progress. He learned from overheard comments that a new type of time transfer was in the process of being assembled here, and that one so large had never been attempted before. If the job was successful, the globe would be carried intact through to his own era for detailed study.

In the meantime another small crew of experts not only explored the ship, taking care not to activate any of its machines, but also made a detailed study of the remains of the crew. Medical men did what they could to discover the cause for the mass death of the space men. And their final verdict was a sudden attack of disease or food poisoning, for there were no wounds.

Three days—four—Travis, weary to his very bones, dragged back from a scouting trip southward and hunched down by fire in the small camp the three field men kept on the heights above the crucial valley. The metallic taste in the air rasped throat and lungs when he breathed deeply. For the past two days the volcanic activity in the north had become more intense. Once the night before they had all been awakened by a display—luckily miles away—during which half a mountain must have blown skyward. Twice torrents of rain had hit, but it was warm rain and the sultriness of the air made conditions now almost tropical. He would be very glad when that fretwork of bars was in place and they could leave this muggy hotbox.

"See anything?" Ross Murdock tossed aside the hide blanket he had pulled about head and shoulders and coughed raspingly as one of the sulphur-tinged breezes curled about them.

"Migration—I think," Travis qualified his report. "The big bison herd is already well south and the hunters are following it."

"Don't like the fireworks, I suppose." Ross nodded to the north. "And I don't blame them. There's a forest burning up there today."

"Seen anything more of the mammoths?"

"Not around here, I was northeast anyway."

"How long before they'll be through down there?" Travis went to look down at the ship. There was a murky haze gathering about the valley and it was spoiling the clearness of view. But men were still aloft on the scaffolding of rods—hurrying to the final capping of the skeleton enclosure about the sphere.

"Ask one of the brains. The other crew—the medics—finished their poking this afternoon. They went through transfer an hour ago. I'd say tomorrow they'll be ready to throw the switch on that gadget. About time. I have a feeling about this place. . . ."

"Maybe rightly." Ashe loomed out of the growing murk. "There's trouble popping to the north." He coughed, and Travis suddenly noted that the mat of wig was missing from the older man's head. He saw that there was a long red mark which could only mark a burn down Ashe's shoulder, crossing the white seam of an earlier scar. Ross, seeing it too, jumped to his feet and turned Ashe toward the light of the fire to inspect that burn closer.

"What did you do—try to play boy on the burning deck?" His voice held an undernote of concern.

"I miscalculated how fast a stand of green timber can burn—when conditions are right. The top of a mountain did blow off last night, and that may have an encore soon. We're moving down nearer to the transfer. And we may have visitors—"

"Hunters? I saw them moving south—"

But Ashe was shaking his head in answer to Travis.

"No, but we may have been too clever about rigging that sonic screen. Those mammoths have been holed up in a small sub-valley to the north. If the hell I'm expecting now breaks loose, sonics won't hold them back, but breaking through such a barrier will make them really wild. They might just charge straight down through here. Kelgarries will have to try his big transfer and quick if that happens."

The scouts reached the floor of the valley in time to see the technicians dropping from the grillwork and hurrying to the time transfer. But they had not come up to the grill when the world went mad. Flame, noise, a thunder in the north, a great up-leap of fire to scorch the underside of lowering clouds. Travis was thrown off his feet as the ground crawled sickeningly. He saw the grid sway about the globe, heard cries and shouts.

"—quake!" A word out of the general clamor

made sense of a sort. The volcanic outburst was being matched by earthquake. Travis stared up at the grid fascinated, expecting every moment to see the rods fly apart, come crashing down upon the dome of the ship. But, strangely enough, though the framework swayed, it did not fall.

In the thickening murk Kelgarries drove his men to the personnel transfer. Travis knew that he should join that line, but he was simply too amazed by the scene to stir. The fog-smoke was denser and out of it arose a shout in a voice he recognized. Getting to his feet, he ran to answer that plea for help.

Ashe lay on the ground. Ross was bending over him, trying to get him to his feet. As Travis blundered up, his spears thrown away, the smoke closed in and set them to a strangled coughing. Travis' sense of direction faltered. Which way was the time transfer? Light ashes drifting through the air blurred air and ground alike—they might have been caught in a snowstorm.

He heard a scream of sheer terror, scaling up. A black shape, larger than the fruit of any nightmare, pounded into sight. The mammoths were charging down-valley as Ashe had feared.

"—get out!" Ross pulled Ashe to the right. Now the older man was between them, stumbling dazedly along.

They skirted the wall of rods about the globe, squeezed through to the ball. A mammoth trumpeted behind them. There was little hope now of reaching the personnel transfer in time and Ashe must have realized that. For he pulled free of the other two and began to move around the ship, one hand on its surface for guide.

Travis guessed his reason—Ashe wanted to find the ladder which led to the open port, use the ship as a refuge. He heard Ashe call, and slipped around behind him to discover that the other held the ladder.

Ross gave his officer a boost, then followed on his heels, while Travis steadied the dangling ladder as best he could. He started to ascend when he saw Ashe, only a dark blot, claw through the port above. He heard again the screeching trumpet of a mammoth and wondered that the beasts had not already smashed into the framework about the ship. Then he in turn was able to scramble through the port, and lay gasping and coughing, the irritation carried in the fog biting into nose and throat tissues.

"Shut it!" Travis was jerked roughly away from the door as someone pushed past him. The outer covering closed with a clang. Now the fog was only a wisp or two, and utter silence took the place of the bedlam outside.

Travis drew a long breath, one which did not this time rasp in his throat. The bluish light from the walls of the ship was subdued, but it was not so dim that he could not see Ashe clearly. The older man lay with his head and shoulders supported by the wall. A bruise was beginning to discolor on his forehead, which was no longer shadowed by any wig. Ross came back from the outer hatch.

"Kind of close quarters here," he commented. "We might as well spread out some."

They went out the inner door of the lock, and

Murdock swung that shut behind them, a move which was perhaps to save their lives.

"In here—" Murdock indicated the nearest door. Those barriers which had been tightly closed on their first visit to the ship had been opened by the technicians. And the cabin beyond contained a furnishing which was a cross between a bunk and a hammock, being both fastened to the wall and swung on straps from the ceiling. Together they guided Ashe to it and got him down, still dazed. Travis had time for no more than a quick glance about when a voice rang down the well of the stair.

"Hey! Who's down there? What's going on?"

They climbed to the control cabin. In front of them stood a wiry young man wearing technician's coveralls, who stared at them wide-eyed.

"Who are you?" he demanded, as he backed away, his fists up to repel an attack.

Travis was completely bewildered until he caught sight of a reflection on the shining surface of the control board—a dirty, three-quarters naked savage. And Ross was his counterpart—the two of them must certainly look like savages to the stranger. Murdock's hands went to his ash-encrusted wig and he peeled it off, a gesture Travis copied. The technician relaxed.

"You're time agents." He made that recognition sound close to an accusation. "What's going on, anyway?"

"General blowup." Ross sat down suddenly and heavily in one of the swinging chairs. Travis leaned against the wall. Here in this silent cabin it was difficult to believe in the disaster and confusion without. "There's a volcanic eruption in progress," Murdock continued. "And the mammoths charged—just before we made it in here—"

The technician started for the stairwell. "We've got to get to the transfer."

Travis caught his arm. "No getting out of the ship now. You can't even see—ash too thick in the air."

"How close were they to taking this ship through?" Ross wanted to know.

"All ready, as far as I know," the technician began, and then added quickly, "d'you mean they'll try to warp her through now—with us inside?"

"It's a chance, just a chance. If the grid survived the quake and the mammoths." Ross's voice was a thin thread, overlaid with a crust of fatigue. "We'll have to wait and see."

"We can *see*—a little." The technician stepped to one of the side panels his hand going to a button there.

Ross moved, coming out of his seat in a spring which rivaled a sabertooth's for speed and deadly purpose. He struck out at the other, sent him sprawling on the floor. But not before the button was pressed home. A plate arose from the board, glowed. Then, over the head of the bewildered and angry technician still on his hands and knees, they caught sight of swirling ash-filled vapor, as if they were looking through a window into the valley.

"You fool!" Ross stood over the technician, and the cold threat Travis had seen in him at their first meeting was very much alive. "Don't touch anything in here!"

"Wise guy, eh?" The technician, his face flushed

and hard, was getting up, his fists ready. "I know what I'm doing—"

"Look—out there!" Travis' cry broke them apart before they tangled.

The fogged picture still held. But there was something else to see there now. It was a build up, bar by bar, square by open square of yellow-green lines of light, possessing the brutal force of lightning but with none of its jagged freedom. The pattern grew fast, dominated the gray of the drifting ash.

"The grid!" The technician broke away from Ross. With his hands on the back of one of the swinging seats, he leaned forward eagerly to watch the vision plate. "They've turned the power on. They're going to try to pull us through!"

The grid continued to glow—to scream with light. They could not watch it now because of its eye-searing brilliance. Then the ship rocked. Another earthquake—or something else? Before Travis could think clearly he was caught up in a fury of sensation for which there had surely never been any name, or any description possible. It was as if his flesh and his mind were at war with each other. He gasped, writhed. The momentary discomfort he had felt when he used the personnel transfer was nothing compared to this wrenching. He tried to find some stability in a dissolving world.

Now he was on the floor. Above him was the window on the outside. He lifted his head slowly, his body felt as if he had been beaten. But that window display—there was no gray now—no ashes falling as snow. All was blue, bright, metallic blue—a blue he knew and that he wanted above him in safety. He staggered up, one hand going out to that promise of blue. But about him still was that feeling of instability.

"Wait!" The technician's fingers caught his wrist in a hard, compelling grasp. He dragged Travis away from the vision plate, tried to push him down in one of the chairs. Ross was beyond, his scarred hand clenched on the edge of a control panel until the seams in the flesh stood out in ugly ridges. His face had lost that expression of cold rage, his expression was intent, wary.

"What's going on?" Ross asked harshly.

It was the technician who gave a sharp order. "Get in that seat! Strap down! If it's what I think, fella—" He shoved Ross back into the nearest chair, and the other obeyed tamely as if he had not been at blows with the man only moments earlier.

"We're through time, aren't we?" Travis still watched that wonderful, peaceful patch of blue sky.

"Sure—we're through. Only how long we're going to stay here . . ." The technician wavered to the third chair, that in which they had discovered the dead pilot days earlier. He sat down with a suddenness close to collapse.

"What do you mean?" Ross's eyes narrowed, his dangerous look was coming back.

"Dragging us through by the energy of the grid did something to the engines here. Don't you feel that vibration, man? I'd say this ship was preparing for a take-off!"

"What?" Travis was half out of his seat. The technician leaned forward, sent him back into the full embrace of the swinging chair with a quick shove. "Don't get any bright ideas about a quick scram out of here, boy. Just look!"

Travis followed the other's pointing finger. The stairwell through which they had climbed to the cabin was now closed.

"Power's on," the other continued. "I'd say we're going out pretty soon."

"We can't!" Travis began and then shivered, knowing the futility of that protest even as he shaped it.

"Anything you can do?" Ross asked, his control once more complete.

The technician laughed, choked, and then waved his hand at the array on the control board. "Just what?" he asked grimly. "I know the use of exactly three little buttons here. We never dared experiment with the rest without dismantling all the installations and tracing them through. I can't stop or start anything. So we're off to the moon and points up, whether we like it or not."

"Anything they can do out there?" Travis turned back to that patch of blue. He knew nothing about the machines, even about the science of mechanics. He could only hope that somewhere, somehow, someone would put an end to this horror which they faced.

The technician looked at him and then laughed again. "They can clear out in a hurry. If there's a backwash when we blast off, a lot of good guys may get theirs."

That vibration, which Travis had sensed on his revival from the strain of the time transport, was growing stronger. It came not only from the walls and flooring of the cabin, but seemingly from the very air he was gulping in quick, shallow breaths. The panic of utter helplessness made him sick, dried his mouth, gripped in twisting pain at his middle.

"How long—?" he heard Ross ask, and saw the technician shake his head.

"Your guess is as good as mine."

"But why? How?" Travis asked hoarsely.

"That pilot, the one they found sitting here . . ." The technician rapped the edge of the control board with his fingers. "Maybe he set automatic controls before he crashed. Then the time transfer—that energy triggered action somewhere. . . . But I'm only guessing."

"Set automatic controls for where?" Ross's tongue swept over his lips as if they were dry.

"Home, maybe. This is it, boys—strap in!"

Travis fumbled with the straps of the seat, pulled them across his body clumsily. He, too, felt that last quiver of addition to the vibration.

Then a hand, an invisible hand as large, as powerful as a mammoth's foot, crushed down upon him. Under his body the seat straightened out into a swaying bed. He was fastened on it, unable to breathe, to think, to do more than feel, endure somehow the pain of flesh and bone under the pressure of that take-off. The blue square was one moment before his aching eyes—and then there was only blackness.

7

TRAVIS came back to consciousness slowly, painfully, aware of a kind of inner bruising before he could assemble his thoughts coherently. He tasted the stale flatness of blood when he tried to swallow and found it hard to focus his eyes. That vision plate which had last been blue was now a dull black. As he moved the slung seat-bed under him swung violently, though the effort he had made was small. Slowly, with caution he raised his body pushing up with both hands.

On another swinging cot lay Ross Murdock, the lower part of his face caked with blood, his eyes closed, his skin a greenish white under the heavy tan and stain. The technician seemed to be in no better state. But under them, around them, the cabin was now quite, devoid of either sound or vibration. Recognizing that, Travis fumbled with the strap across his middle, tried to get up.

This attempt brought disastrous results. His efforts drove him away from his support, right enough. But his feet did not touch the floor. Instead he plunged out, weightless, to bring up against the edge of the main control board with force enouoh to raise a little yelp of pain. Panic-stricken, he held on to the board, pulling himself along until he could reach the technician. He tried to rouse the other, his methods growing rougher when they did not appear to be answered by any signs of returning consciousness.

Finally the man groaned, turned his head, and opened his eyes. As awareness grew in their depths, so did surprise and fear.

"What—what happened?" The words were slurred. "You hurt?"

Travis drew the back of his hand across mouth and chin, brought it away clotted with blood. He must look as bad as Ross.

"Can't walk." He introduced the foremost problem of the moment. "Just—float. . . ."

"Float?" repeated the technician, then he struggled up, unfastened his belt. "Then we are *are* through—out of gravity! We're in space!"

Jumbled fragments of articles he had read arose out of Travis' memory. Free of gravity—no up, down—no weight— He was nauseated, his head spinning badly, but keeping hold of the board he worked his way past the technician to Ross. Murdock was already stirring, and as Travis laid hand on his seat he moaned, his fingers sweeping aimlessly across his chest as if to soothe some hurt there.

Travis gently caught the other's bloody chin, shaking his head slowly from side to side as the gray eyes opened.

". . . and that's it, we're out!" Case Renfry, the technician, shook his head at the flood of questions from the time scouts. "Listen, fellas, I was loaned to this project to help with the breakdown appraisal. I can't fly any ship, let alone this one—so it must be on automatic controls."

"Set by the dead pilot. Then it should go back to his base," Travis suggested gloomily.

"You are forgetting one thing." Ross sat up with care, keeping firm hold on his mooring with both hands. "That pilot's base is twelve thousand years or so in the past. They warped us through time before we took off—"

"And we can't go home?" Travis demanded again of the technician.

"I wouldn't try meddling with any key on that board," Renfry said, shaking his head. "If we're flying on automatic controls, the best thing is to keep on to the destination and then see what we can do."

"Only there are a few other things to consider— such as food, water, air supplies," Travis pointed out.

"Yes—air," Ross underlined with chilling soberness. "How long might we be on the way?"

Renfry grinned weakly. "Your guess is as good as mine. The air supply is all right—I think. They had a going plant in the ship and Stefferds said it was in perfect working order. Keep it fresh by some species of algae in a sealed section. You can look in at it but you can't contaminate the place. And they breathed about the same mixture as we do. But as to food and water—we'd better look around. Three of us to feed . . ."

"Four! There's Ashe!" Ross, forgetting where he was, tried to jump free of his seat and swam forward in a tangle of flailing legs and arms until Renfry drew him down.

"Take it easy, mighty easy, fella. Hit the wrong button while you're putting on a dive act that way and we could be worse off than we are. Who's Ashe?"

"Our section chief. We stowed him in a cabin down below, he had had a bad knock on the head."

Travis aimed for the well leading to the center section of the globe. He overshot, bounced back, and was thankful when his fingers closed on the bar of its cover. They got it open and made their way clumsily in a direction Travis still thought of—in spite of the evidence of his eyes—as "down."

To descend into the heart of the ship required an agility which was a torment to their bruised and aching bodies. But when they at last reached the cabin they found Ashe still safely stowed in the bunk, far better tended against the force of the take-off than they had been. For only his peaceful face showed above a thick mass of a jelly substance which filled the interior of the bunk-hammock.

"He'll be all right. That's the stuff they keep in their lifeboats to patch up the injured—saved my life once," Ross identified. "A regular cure for anything."

"How do you know so much?" Renfry began, and then, his eyes wonderingly on Ross, he added, "why—you must be the guy who was with the Reds on that ship they were stripping!"

"Yes. But I'd like to know a little more about this one. Food—water. . . ."

They went exploring in Renfry's wake, discovering adaption to weightlessness a hard job, but determined to learn what they could of the best, and the worst, of their predicament. The technician had been all through the ship and now he displayed to them the air-renewal unit, the engine room, and the crew's quarters. They made a detailed examination of what could only be a mess cabin combined with kitchen. It was a cramped space in which no more than four men—or man-like beings—could fit at one time.

Travis frowned at the rows of sealed containers racked in the cupboards. He extracted one, shook it near his ear, and was rewarded by a gurgle which made him run a dry tongue over his blood-stained lips. There must be liquid of a sort inside, and he could not remember now when he had had a really satisfying drink.

"This is water—if you want a drink." Renfry brought a Terran canteen out of a corner. "We had four of these on board, used 'em while we were working."

Travis reached for the metal bottle, but did not uncap it after all. "Still have all four?" Perhaps more than any of the rest on board he knew the value of water, the disaster of not having it.

Renfry brought them out, shaking each. "Three sound full. This one's about half—maybe a little less."

"We'll have to go on rations."

"Sure," the technician agreed. "Think there're some concentrate food tablets here, too. You fellas have any of those?"

"Ashe still had his supply bag with him, didn't he?" Travis asked Ross.

"Yes. And we'd better see how many of the tablets we can find."

Travis looked at the alien container which had gurgled. At the moment he would have given a great deal to be able to force the lid, to drink its contents and ease both thirst and hunger.

"We may have to come to trying these." Renfry took the container from the scout, filled it back into the holder space.

"I'd guess we'll have to try a lot of things before this trip is over—if it ever is. Right now I'd like to try a bath, or at least a wash." Ross surveyed his own scratched, half-naked, and very dirty body with marked disfavor.

"That you can have. Come on."

Again Renfry played guide, bringing them to a small cubbyhole beyond the mess cabin. "You stand on that—maybe you can hold yourself in place with those." He pointed to some rods set in the wall. "But get your feet down on that round plate and then press the circle in the wall."

"Then what happens? You roast or broil?" Travis inquired with suspicion.

"No—this really works. We tried it on a guinea pig yesterday. Then Harvey Bush used it after he upset a can of oil all over him. It's rather like a shower."

Ross jerked at the ties of his disreputable kilt and

kicked off his sandals, his movements sending him skidding from wall to wall. "All right. I'm willing to try." He got his feet on the plate, holding himself in position by the rods, and then pressed the circle. Mist curled from under the edge of the floor plate, enveloped his legs, rose steadily. Renfry pushed shut the door.

"Hey!" protested Travis, "he's being gassed!"

"It's okay!" Ross's voice, disembodied, came from beyond. "In fact—it's better than okay!"

When he came out of the fogged cubby a few minutes later, the grime and much of the stain were gone from his body. Moreover, scratches which had been raw and red were now only faint pinkish lines. Ross was smiling.

"All the comforts of home. I don't know what that stuff is, but it peals you right down to your second layer of hide and makes you like it. The first good thing we've found in this mousetrap."

Travis shucked his kilt a little more slowly. He didn't relish being shut into that gassy box, but neither did he enjoy the present state of his person. Gingerly he stepped, or skipped, onto the floor disk, got his feet flattened on its surface, and pressed the circle, holding his breath as the gassy substance puffed up to enfold him.

The stuff was not altogether a gas, he discovered, for it had more body than any vapor. Rather, it was as if he were immersed in a flood of frothy bubbles which rubbed and slicked across his skin with the even pressure of a vigorous toweling. Grinning, he relaxed and, closing his eyes, ducked his head under the surface. He felt the smooth swish across his face, drawing the sting out of scratches and the ache out of his bruises and bumps.

When the bubbles ebbed and Travis stepped out of the cubby, he was met by a changed Ross. The latter was just hitching up over his broad shoulders the upper part of a tight, blue-green suit which clung to his body, modeling every muscle as he moved. One piece, its stocking covering for legs and feet were soled with a thick sponge which cushioned each step. Ross picked another bundle of blue-green from the floor and tossed it to the Apache.

"Compliments of the house," he said. "I certainly never thought I'd want to wear one of these again."

"Their uniforms?" Travis remembered the dead pilot. "What is this—silk?" He rubbed his hand over the sleek surface of a fabric he could not identify, and was attracted by the play of color—blue, green, lavender. It rippled from one shade ot another as the material moved.

"Yes. It has its good points, all right—insulated against cold and heat, for one thing. For another, it can be traced."

Travis paused, his arm half through the right sleeve. "Traced?"

"Well, I was trailed over about fifty miles of pretty rugged territory because I was wearing one like this. And they tried to get at me mentally, too, when I had it on. Went to sleep one night and woke up heading right back to the boys who wanted to collect me."

Travis stared, but it was plain Ross meant every word he said. Then the Apache glanced down again at the silky stuff he was wearing, with an impulse to strip it off. Yet Murdock in spite of his story, was fastening the studs which ran from one shoulder to the other hip of his own garment.

"If we were in the right time, I wouldn't touch this with a fifty-foot pole," Ross continued, smiling wryly. "But, seeing as how we are some thousands of years removed from the rightful owners, I'll take the chance. As I said, these suits do have some points in their favor."

Travis snapped his own studs together. The material felt good, smooth, a little warm, almost as soothing as the foam bubbles which had scoured and energized his tired body. He was willing to chance wearing the uniform; it was infinitely better than the hide garment he had discarded.

They were learning to navigate through weightlessness. The usual form of progress approached swimming, and they found convenient handholds to draw them along. If Travis could forget that the ship was boring on into the unknown, their present lodging had a lot to recommend it. But when the four of them gathered in the control cabin an hour or so later, they prepared to consider the major problem with what objectivity they could summon.

Ashe, alertly himself again, fresh from the healing of the aliens' treatment, held the leadership by unspoken consent. Only it was to Renfry that the three time scouts looked for hope. The technician had little to offer.

"The pilot must have set the ship's controls on

some type of homing device just before he died. I'm just guessing at this, you understand, but it is the only explanation to make sense now. When we explored here, my chief, working from what he knew of the tape records from the Russian headquarters, traced three installations: the one giving outside vision," he began, tapping lightly on the plate which had been blue for those few precious moments before their involuntary take-off. "Another which is the inside com system connecting speakers all over the ship. And a third—this." He pressed a lever to its head in a slot. Three winks of light showed on the board and out of the air above their heads came a sound which might have been a word in an unknown tongue."

"And what *is* that?" Ashe watched the lights with interest.

"Guns! We have four ports open now, and a weapon in each ready to fire. It was the chief's guess that this was—is—a small military scout, or police patrol ship." He clicked the lever back into place and the lights were gone.

"Not very helpful now," Ross commented. "What about the chances for getting back home?"

Renfry shrugged. "Not a chance that I can see so far. Frankly, I'm afraid to do any poking around these controls while we're in space. There is too good a chance of stopping and not getting started again—either forward or back."

"That makes sense. So we'll just have to keep on going to whatever port for which your controls are now set?"

Renfry nodded. "Not *my* controls, though, sir.

This—all of this—is far advanced, and different—beyond our planes. Maybe, if I had time, and we were safely on ground, I could discover how the engines tick, but what makes them do so would still be another problem.''

''Atomic fuel?''

''Even that I can't say. The engines are completely sealed. That sealing may be atomic shielding, we didn't dare pry too far.''

''And home port may be anywhere in the universe,'' mused Ashe. ''They had some type of distance-time jump—voyages couldn't have lasted centuries.''

Renfry was studying the banks of buttons and levers with an expression of complete exasperation. ''They could have every gadget in a fiction writer's imagination, sir, and we wouldn't know it—until the thing did or didn't work!''

''Quite a prospect.'' Ashe got up with the careful motions of a novice in no-weight. ''I think a detailed exploration of the rest of our present home is now in order.''

There were three of the small living cabins, each equipped with two bunk-hammocks. And by experimenting with the wall panels they discovered clothing, personal effects of the crew. Travis did not like like to empty those shallow cupboards and handle those possessions of dead men. But he did his share during the hunt for some clue which might mean the difference between life and death for the present passengers. He had opened a last small cavity in one locker when he caught a promising glitte . He picked up the object and found himself holding a rectangle of some slick material with the texture of glass. It was milky white, blank when he picked it up. But the chill of the first touch faded as he turned it over curiously. The rim was bordered in a band of tiny flashing bits of yellow which might be gem stones—framing blankness instead of a picture.

A picture! If he could hold a picture of a far place—what sort would it be? Family—home—friends? He watched the plain surface within the border. Plain—? There *was* something there! Color was seeping up to the surface, spreading; outlines were becoming solid. Bewildered, almost frightened, Travis studied that changing scene.

He did have a picture now. And one he knew. It was an entirely familiar scene—a stretch of desert and mountains. Why, he might be standing on the cliffs looking toward Red Horse Canyon! He wanted to throw the thing from him. How could an alien who lived twelve thousand years ago carry among his belongings a picture of the country Travis knew as home? It was unbelievable—unreal!

"What is it, son?" Ashe's hand was real on his arm, Ashe's voice warm through the chill congealing inside him as he continued to stare at the thing he held, the thing which, in spite of its familiar beauty, was wrong, terrible. . . .

"Picture . . ." he mumbled. "Picture of my home—here."

"What?" Ashe stopped closer and gave an exclamation, took the block out of Travis's hands. The younger man wiped his sweating palms down his thighs, trying to wipe away the touch of that weird picture.

But, as he watched the desert scene, he cried out. For it was fading away, the colors were absorbed in the original white. The outlines of cliffs and mountains were gone. Ashe held the plaque up in both of his hands. And now there was a new stirring in the depths, a murky flowing as again a scene grew into sharp brilliance.

Only this was not the desert, but a stand of tall, green trees Travis recognized as pines. Below them was a strand of gray-white sand, and beyond the pound of waves lashing high in foam against fanged rocks. Above that restless water white birds hung.

"Safeharbor!" Ashe sat down suddenly on the bunk and the picture shook as his hands trembled. "That's the beach by my home in Maine—in Maine, I tell you! Safeharbor, Maine! But how did this get here?" His expression was one of dazed bewilderment.

"To me it showed my home also," Travis said slowly. "And now to you another scene. Perhaps to the man who once lived in this cabin it also showed his home. This is a magic thing, I think. Not of the magic which your people have harnessed to do their will, nor of the magic of my Old Ones either." Somehow the thought that this object bewildered the white man as much as it did him took away a little of the fear. Ashe raised his eyes from the scene of shore and sea to meet Travis'. Slowly he nodded.

"You may be guessing, but I'll stake a lot on your guess being right. What they knew, these people—

what wonders they knew! We must learn all we can, follow them."

Travis laughed shakily. "Follow them we are, Doctor Ashe. About the learning—well, we shall see."

8

A FIGURE edged along the narrow corridor, his cushioned feet barely touching the floor. In the timeless interior of the spaceship where there was no change between day and night, Travis had had to wait a long time for this particular moment. His brown hands, too thin nowadays, played with the fastening of his belt. Under that was a gnawing ache which never left him now.

They had stretched their water supply with strict rationing, and the concentrate tablets the same way. But tomorrow—or in the next waking period they would arbitrarily label "tomorrow"—they would have only four of those small squares. And Travis was keenly aware of not only that indisputable fact but of something which Ross had said that day when they had argued out the need for experiment with alien food supplies.

"Case Renfry," the younger time agent had pointed out the obvious, "is certainly not going to be your tester. If we are ever going to be able to find out what makes this bus tick and get it started home again, he's the one to do it. And, chief"—he had then turned upon Ashe—"you've the best brain— it's up to you to help him. Maybe somewhere in this loot we've found you can locate a manual, or a do-it-yourself tape that'll give us a fair break."

They had been pulling over the material they had found in the cabins. Objects such as the disappearing picture were set aside on the hope that Ashe, with his archaeologist's training in the penetration of age-old mysteries, might understand them through study.

"Which," Ross had continued, "leaves the food problem up to a volunteer—me."

Travis had remained quiet, but he had also made plans. He had already followed Ross's reasoning to a logical end, but his conclusion differed from Murdock's. Of the four men on board he, not Murdock, was certainly the most expendable. And the history of his people testified to the fact that Apaches possessed the toughest of digestive apparatus. They had been able to live off the natural products of a land where other races starved. So—he was now engaged in his own private project.

Last sleep period he had tackled the first container chosen from the supply cupboard. The one which had sloshed when shaken. He had swallowed two large mouthfuls of a sickly sweet substance with the consistency of stew. And, while the taste had not been pleasant, Travis had suffered no discomfort afterward. Now he chose a small round can, prying off the lid quickly while listening for any warning from the corridor.

He had left Ross asleep in the small cabin they shared, had looked in upon Renfry and Ashe before he made this trek. There was so little time and he had to wait a reasonable period between each tasting.

Travis wanted a drink, but he knew better than to take one. He had palmed his concentrate tablet at the last "meal," held the canteen to his mouth but not drunk, keeping his stomach empty. Now he studied his new selection with disgust.

A brown jelly, it quivered slightly with the movement of the cylinder in his hand, its surface reflecting the light. Using the edge of the lid as an improvised spoon, Travis ladled a portion into his mouth. Unlike the stew the stuff had little flavor, though he did not relish the greasy feel on his tongue. He swallowed, took a second helping. Then he chose a third sample—a square box. He would wait. If there were no ill effects from the jelly—then this. If he could prove four or five of these different containers held food the Terrans could stomach, they might have enough to outlast the voyage.

He did not return to his bunk. The magnetic bottoms of each container clung to the surface of the table, just as the thick soles of his suit feet clung to the walking surfaces in the ship when he planted them firmly. They had all adapted in a measure to the lack of gravity and the actual conditions of space flight. But Travis had a struggle to conceal his dislike of the ship itself, of the confinement forced upon them. And now, to sit alone brought him a fraction of comfort, for he dared to relax that strict control.

He had enjoyed the venture into time. The prehistoric world had been an open wilderness he could understand. But the ship was different. It seemed to him that the taint of death still clung to its small cabins, the narrow corridors and ladders, that the very alienness of it was a menace far more acute than a sabertooth or a mammoth in a rocking charge.

Once he had believed that he wanted to know more about the Old Ones. He had wanted to probe the mysteries which could be deduced from bits of broken pottery or an arrowhead pried from a dust-filled crevice in a cave. But those Old Ones had been distantly akin to him—those who had built this ship were not. For a moment or two his claustrophobia welled up, shaking his control, making him want to batter the walls about him with his fists, to beat his way out of this shell into the light, the air—freedom.

But outside these walls there was no light, no air, and only the freedom of vacuum—or of the mysterious hyperspace which canceled the distance between the stars. Travis fought his imagination. He could not face that picture of the ship hanging in an emptiness where perhaps there were not even the frigid points of light to mark the stars—where there was nothing solid and stable.

The travelers could only hope that sometime they would reach the home port for which the dying alien pilot had set controls. But that course had been set twelve thousand—perhaps more—years ago. What port would they find waiting beyond the wall of time? Twelve—fifteen thousand years. . . . These were figures too great for the normal comprehension of ordinary man. At that time on earth, the first mud-walled villages had not yet been built, nor the first patch of grain sown to turn man from a wandering hunter to the householder, the landowner. What had the Apache been then—and the white man? Roving hunters with skill in spear and knife and the running down of game. Yet it was at that time that these aliens had produced this ship, voyaged space, not only between the planets of a single system, but from star to star!

Travis tried to think of their future, but his thoughts kept sliding back to the pressing urge to be in the open. He yearned to stand under the sun with wind—yes, even a desert wind hot and laden with grit—blowing against him. That longing was as acute as a pain—a pain!

His hands went to his middle. A sudden thrust of pure agony had rent him and it was not born out of any homesickness. The cramping was physical and very real. He bent half double, trying to ease that hot clawing in his insides as the cabin misted before his eyes. Then the stab was gone, and he straightened—until it caught him again. This was it. His luck at his second attempt with the alien food was bad.

Somehow he got to his feet, lurched against the table as a third bout of cramps caught him. The torture ebbed, leaving his hands and face wet. And in the few moments before the next pang he made it halfway along the corridor, reaching the haven he sought just as his outraged stomach finally revolted.

Travis would not have believed that two mouthfuls of a greasy jelly could so weaken a man. He pulled his spent body back to the mess cabin, dropping limply into a chair. More than anything now he wanted water, to cleanse the foulness from his mouth, to slake the burning in his throat. The canteens mocked him for he dare not take one up, knowing just how little of the precious liquid still remained.

For a while he hunched over the table, weakly glad of his freedom from pain. Then he drew the can of jelly to him. This must be marked poisonous. Only two containers had been tested—and how many more would prove impossible?

Only five concentrate tablets were left, counting the one he had hidden that day. Nothing was going to multiply that five into ten—or into two hundred. If they were to survive the voyage of unknown duration, they *must* use some of this other food. But Travis could not control the shaking of his hands as he worked to free the lid of the square box. Maybe he was rushing things, taking another sample so soon after the disastrous effects of the other. But he knew that if he did not, right here and now, he might not be able to force himself to the third attempt later.

The lid came free and he saw inside dry squares of red. To his questing finger these had the texture of something between bread and a harder biscuit. He raised the can to sniff. For the first time the odor was faintly familiar. Tortillas paper-thin and crisp from the baking had an aroma not unlike this. And because the cakes did arouse pleasant memories, Travis bit into one with more eagerness than he would have believed possible moments earlier.

The stuff crumbled between his teeth like corn bread, and he thought the flavor was much the same, in spite of the unusual color. He chewed and swallowed. And the mouthful, dry as it was, appeared to erase the burning left by the jelly. The taste was so good that he ventured to take more than a few bites, finishing the first cake and then a second. Finally, still holding the box in one hand, he slumped lower in his seat, his eyes closing as his worn body demanded rest.

He was riding. There was the entrance to Red Horse Canyon, and the scent of juniper was in the air. A bird flew up—his eyes followed that free flight. An eagle! The bird of power, ascending far up into a cloudless sky. But suddenly the sky was no longer blue, but black with a blackness not born of normal night. It was black, and caught in it were stars. The stars grew swiftly larger—because he was being drawn up into the blackness where there were only stars. . . .

Travis opened heavy-lidded eyes, looked up foggily at a blue figure. Looming over him was a thin, drawn face, slight hollows marking the cheeks, dark smudges under cold gray eyes.

"Ross!" The Apache lifted his head from his arm, wincing at the painful crick in his back.

The other sat down across the table, glanced from the array of supply containers to Travis and back again.

"So this is what you've been doing!" There was accusation in his tone, almost a note of outrage.

"You said yourself it was a job for the most expendable."

"Trying to be a hero on the quiet!" Now the accusation was plain and hot.

"Not much of a one." Travis rested his chin on his fist and considered the containers lined up before him. "I've sampled three so far—exactly three."

Ross's eyelids flickered down. His usual control was back in place, though Travis did not doubt the antagonism was still eating at him.

"With what results?"

"Number one"—Travis indicated the proper can—"too sweet, kind of a stew—but it stays with you in spite of the taste. This is number two." He tapped the tin of brown jelly. "I'd say its only use was to get rid of wolves. This"—he cradled the can of red cakes—"is really good."

"How long have you been at it?"

"I tried one last sleep period, two this."

"Poison, eh?" Ross picked up the tin of jelly, inspecting its contents.

"If it isn't poison, it puts up a good bluff," Travis shot back a little heatedly, stung by the suggestion of skepticism.

Ross set it down. "I'll take your word for it," he conceded. "What about this little number?" He had arisen to stand before the cupboard, and now he turned, holding a shallow, round container. The secret of its fastening was harder to solve, but when it was open at last they looked at some small balls in yellow sauce.

"D'you know, those might just be beans," Ross observed. "I've yet to see any service ship where beans in some form or other didn't turn up on the menu. Let's see if they eat like beans." He scooped up a good mouthful and chewed thoughtfully. "Beans—no—I'd say they taste more like cabbage—which had been spiced up a bit. But not bad, not bad at all!"

Travis found himself nursing a small wicked desire to have the cabbage-beans do their worst to Ross, not with as devastating results as the jelly—he wouldn't wish *that* on anyone! But if they would just make themselves felt enough to prove to Murdock that food testing was not as easy as all that. . . .

"Waiting for them to turn me inside out?" Ross grinned.

Travis flushed and then the stain spread and deepened on his cheeks as he realized how he had given himself away. He pushed the cracker-bread to one side and got up to select with inward—if not outward—defiance a tall cylinder which sloshed as he pried at its cap.

"Misery loves company," Ross continued. "What does that smell like?"

Travis had been encouraged by his discovery of the bread. He sniffed hopefully at the cone opening and then snatched the holder away from his nose as a white froth began to puff out.

"Maybe you have the push-button soap," Ross commented unhelpfully. "Give the stuff a lick, fella, you have only one stomach to lose for your country."

Travis, so goaded, licked—suspicious and expecting something entirely unpalatable. But, to his surprise, though it was sweet, the froth was not so sickly as the stew had been. Rather, the result on the tongue was refreshing, carrying satisfaction for his craving for water. He gulped a bigger mouthful and sat waiting, a little tensely, for fireworks to begin inside him.

"Good?" Ross inquired. "Well, your luck can't be rotten all the time."

"This luck is mixed." Travis capped the foam which had continued to boil wastefully from the bottle. "We're alive—and we're still traveling."

"Traveling is right. A little more information as to our destination would be useful and comforting—or the reverse."

"The world the builders of this ship owned can't be too different from ours," Travis repeated observations made earlier by Ashe. "We can breathe their air without discomfort, and maybe eat some of their food."

"Twelve thousand years. . . . D'you know, I can say that but I can't make it mean anything real." Ross's hostility had either vanished or been submerged. "You say the words but you can't stretch your imagination to make them picture something for you—or do you know what I mean?" he challenged.

Travis, rasped on an ancient raw spot, schooled down some heat before he replied. "A little. I did four years at State U. We don't wear our blankets and feathers *all* the time."

Ross glanced up, a flicker of puzzlement in those cold gray eyes.

"I didn't mean it like that—for what it's worth." Then he smiled and for the first time there was nothing superior or sardonic in that expression. "Want the whole truth, fella? I picked up what education I had before I went into the Project the hard way—no State U. But you studied the chief's racket—archaeology—didn't you?"

"Yes."

"So—what does twelve thousand years mean to you? You deal with time in big doses, don't you?"

"That's a long span on our world, jumps one clear back to the cave period."

"Yeah—before they put up the pyramids of Egypt—before they learned to read and write. Well, twelve thousand years ago, these blue boys had the stars for theirs. But I'm betting they haven't kept them! There hasn't been a single country on our world, not even China, that has had a form of civilization lasting that long. Up they climb and then—" he snapped his fingers. "It's kaput for them, and another top dog takes over the power. So maybe when we get to this port Renfry believes we're homing for, we'll find nothing, or else someone else waiting for us there. You can bet one way or another and have a good chance of winning on either count. Only, if we do find nothing—then maybe our number's up for sure."

Travis had to accept the logic of that. Suppose they did come into a port which had ceased to exist, set down on a strange world from which they could not lift again because they had not the skill to pilot the ship. They would be exiles for the rest of their lives in a space uncharted by their kind.

"We're not dead yet," Travis said.

Ross laughed "In spite of all our efforts? No—that's our private battle cry, I think. As long as a man's alive he's going to keep kicking. But it would be good to know just how long we're going to be shut up in this ship." His usual half flippancy of tone thinned over that last as if his carefully cultivated self-sufficiency was beginning to show the slimmest of cracks.

In the end their experiments with the food were partially successful. The crackers Travis continued to label "corn"; the foam and Ross's cabbage-beans could be digested by the interior apparatus of a human being without difficulty. And they added to that list a sticky paste with the consistency of jam and a flavor approaching bacon, and another cake-like object which, though it had a sour tang that puckered the mouth, was still edible. Greatly daring, Travis tapped the aliens' water supply and drank. Though the liquid had a metallic aftertaste which the drinker could not relish, it was not harmful.

In addition the younger members of the involuntary crew made themselves useful in the cautious investigations carried on by Ashe and Renfry. The technician was in an almost constant state of frustration during the hours he spent in the control cabin trying to study machines he dared not activate or dismantle for the fuller examination he longed to make. Travis was seated behind him one morning—at least it was ten o'clock by Renfry's watch, their only method of time-keeping—when there *was* a change to report, to report and take action on.

A shrill buzz pierced the usual silence, beeping what must be a warning. Renfry grabbed at the small mike of the ship's com circuit.

"Strap down!" He rasped the order with rising excitement. "There's an alert sounding here—we may be coming in to land. Strap down!"

Travis grabbed at the protecting bands on his chair. Below they must be scrambling for the bunks. There was vibration again—he was sure he could not mistake that. The ship no longer felt inert and drifting—she was coming alive.

What followed was again beyond his powers of description. The action came in two parts, the first a queasy whirl of sensation not far removed from what they had experienced when the ship had been whirled through the time transfer. Limp from that, Travis lay back, watching the vision plate which had been blank for so long. And when his eyes caught what was not appearing there, he gave a cry of recognition.

"That's the sun!"

A point of blazing yellow set a beacon in the black of space.

"A sun," Renfry corrected. "We've made the big hop. Now it's the homestretch—into the system. . . ."

That blaze of yellow-red was already sliding away from the plate. Travis had an impression that the ship must be slowly rotating. Now that the brighter glare of the sun was gone he could pick up a smaller dot, far smaller than the star which nurtured it. That held steady on the plate.

"Something tells me, boy," Renfry said in a

small and hesitant voice, "that's where we're going."

"Earth?" A warm surge of hope spread through Travis.

"An earth maybe—but not ours."

9

"WE'RE down." Renfry's voice, thin, harsh, broke the silence of the control cabin. His hands moved to the edge of the panel of levers and buttons before him, fell helplessly on it. Though he had had nothing to do with that landing, he seemed drained by some great effort.

"Home port?" Travis got the words out between dry lips. The descent had not been as nerve- and body-wracking as their take-off from his native world, but it had been bad enough. Either the aliens' bodies were better atuned to the tempo of their ships, or else one acquired, through painful experience, a conditioning to such wrenching.

"How would I know?" Renfry flared, plainly eaten by his own frustration.

Their window on the outside world, the vision

plate, did mirror sky again. But not the normal Terran sky with its blue blaze which Travis knew and longed to see again. This was a blue closer to green, assuming the hue of the turquoise mined in the hills. There was something cold, inimical in that sky.

Cutting up into the open space was a structure which gave off a metallic glint. But the smooth sweep of those dull red surfaces ended in a jagged splinter, raw against the blue-green, plainly marking a ruin.

Travis unfastened his seat straps and stumbled to his feet, his body once more adjusting clumsily to the return of gravity. As much as he had come to dislike the ship, to want his freedom from it, at this moment he had no desire to emerge under that turquoise sky and examine the ruin pictured on the plate. And just because he did have that reluctance, he fought against it by going.

In the end they all gathered at the space lock while Renfry mastered the fastening, then went on to the outer door. The technician glanced back over his shoulder.

"Helmets fastened?" His voice boomed hollowly inside the sphere now resting on Travis' shoulders and made a part of him by a close-fitting harness. Ashe had discovered those and had tested them, preparing for this time when they had to dare a foray into the unknown. The bubble was equipped with no cumbersome oxygen tanks. It worked on no principle Renfry was able to discover, but the aliens had used these and the Terrans must trust to their efficiency now.

The outer port swung back into the skin of the

ship. Renfry kicked out the landing ladder, turned to back down it. But each of them, as he emerged from the globe, glanced quickly around.

What lay below was a wide sweep of hard white surface which must cover miles of territory. This was broken at intervals by a series of structures of the dull red, metallic material set in triangles and squares. In the center of each of those was a space marked with black rings. None of the red structures was whole, and the landing field—if that was what it was—had the sterile atmosphere of a place long abandoned.

"Another ship. . . ." Ashe's arm swung up, his voice came to Travis through the helmet com.

There was a second of the globes, right enough, reposing in one of the building-cornered squares perhaps a quarter of a mile away. And beyond that Travis spotted a third. But nowhere was there any sign of life. He felt wind, soft, almost caressing, against his bare hands.

They descended the ladder and stood in a group at the foot of their own ship, a little uncertain as to what to do next.

"Wait!" Renfry caught at Ashe. "Something moved—over there!"

They had found weapons in the ship; now they drew those odd guns, twin to the one Ross had had when Travis had first met him. The wind blew, a fragment of long-dead vegetation balled before it, caught against the globe and then was whirled away in a dreary dance.

But out of an opening at the foot of the red tower nearest to them something was issuing. And Travis, watching that coil snapping straight for them, froze. A snake? A snake unwinding to such a length that its reaching head was approaching their stand while the end of its tail still lay within the ruin where it denned?

He took aim at that swaying coil. Then Renfry's hand struck his wrist pads, knocking up the barrel of the blaster. And in that moment the Apache saw what the other had noticed first, that the snake was not a thing of flesh, skin, supple bones, but of some manufactured material.

More movement was continuing to issue in a mechanical writhing from the door through which the snake had crawled. This newcomer strode forward by jerks, paused, came on, as if compelled to advance against the dictates of ancient fabric and long wear. The thing was vaguely manlike in form, in that it advanced on stilt legs. But it had four upper appendages now folded against its central bulk, and where the head should have been there was a nodding stalk resembling the antennae of a com unit.

Its jerky walk with the many pauses conveyed more and more a sense of internal discord, of rust and wear, and the deterioration of time. How much time? The four Terrans stepped away from the ship, giving free passage to the strange partners from the tower.

"Robots!" Ross said suddenly. "They're robots! But what are they going to do?"

"Refuel, I think." Ashe rather than Renfry answered that.

"You've hit it!" The technician pushed forward. "But do they have fuel—now?"

"We'd better hope there is some left." Ashe sounded bleak. "I'd say we aren't supposed to stay here—better get back on board."

The threat of being trapped here, of locked controls raising the ship and leaving them marooned, induced a wave of something close to panic in all three hearers. They raced to the ladder, began to climb. But when they reached the air lock, Renfry remained at the open door, retailing the movements of the robots.

"I think that animated pipeline's been connected—underneath. Can't see what the walker's doing—maybe he just stands by in case of trouble. And there's something coming through the hose—you can see it swell! We're taking on whatever we're supposed to have!"

"A fueling station." Ashe looked out over the wide stretch of crumbling towers and checkerboard landing spaces. "But see the size of this place. It must have been constructed to handle hundreds, even thousands, of ships. And since they couldn't *all* be in to refuel at the same time, that presupposes a fleet"—he drew a deep breath of wonder—"a fleet almost beyond comprehension. We were right—this civilization was galaxy-wide. Maybe it spread to the next galaxy."

But Travis' eyes rested on the splintered cap of the tower from which the robots had come. "By the looks no one has been here for some time," he observed.

"Machines," Renfry answered, "will go on working until they run down. I'd say that walking one down there is close to its final stop. We triggered some impulse when we landed on the right spot. The robots were activated to do their job—maybe their last job. How long since they worked the last time? This may have kept going for a long part of that twelve thousand years you're always talking about—an empire dying slowly. But I wouldn't try to measure the time. These aliens knew machinery, and their alloys are better than our best.''

''I'd like to see the interior of one of those towers,'' Ashe said wistfully. ''Maybe they kept records, had something we could understand to explain it all.''

Renfry shook his head. ''Wouldn't dare try it. We might raise before you got inside the door. Ahh—the walker is going back now. I'd say get ready for take-off.''

They made tight the open port, the inner door of the space lock. Renfry, out of habit, went on up to the control cabin. But the other three took to their bunks. There was a waiting period and then once more the blast into space. This time they did not lose consciousness and endured until they were once more in space.

''Now what?'' Hours later they squeezed into the mess cabin to hold a rather aimless conference concerning the future. Since no one had anything more than guesses to offer, none of them answered Renfry's question.

''I read a book once,'' Ross said suddenly with the slightly embarrassed air of one admitting to a minor social error, ''that had a story in it about some Dutch sea captain who swore he'd get around the horn in one of those old-time sailing ships. He called up the

Devil to help him and he never got home—just went on sailing through the centuries.''

"The Flying Dutchman," Ashe identified.

"Well, we haven't called up any Devil," Renfry remarked.

"Haven't we?" Travis had spoken his thoughts, without realizing until they all stared at him that he had done so aloud.

"Your Devil being?" Ashe prompted.

"We were trying to get knowledge out of this ship—and it wasn't our kind of knowledge," he floundered a little, attempting to put into words what he now believed.

"Scavengers getting their just deserts?" Ashe summed up. "If you follow that line of reasoning, yes, you have a point. The forbidden fruit of knowledge. That was an idea planted so long ago in mankind's conscience that it lingers today as guilt."

"Planted," Ross repeated the word thoughtfully, "planted. . . ."

"Planted!" Travis echoed, his mind making one of those odd jumps in sudden understanding of which he had only recently become conscious. "By whom?"

Then glancing around at the alien ship which was both their transport and their prison, he added softly, "By these people?"

"They didn't want us to know about them." Ross's words came in a rush. "Remember what they did to that Red time base—traced it all the way forward and destroyed it in every era. Suppose they *did* have contacts with primitive man on our world—planted ideas—or gave them such a terrifying lesson at one time or other that the memory of it was buried in all their descendants?"

"There are other tales beside your Flying Dutchman, Ross," Ashe squirmed a little in his seat. None of the chairs in the ship was exactly fitted to the human frame or provided comfort for the modern passengers. "Prometheus and the fire—the man who dared to steal the knowledge of the gods for the use of mankind and suffered eternally thereafter for his audacity, though his fellows benefited. Yes, there are clues to back such a theory, faint ones." His eagerness grew as he spoke. "Maybe—just maybe—we'll find out!"

"The supply port was long deserted," Travis pointed out. "There may be nothing left of their empire anywhere."

"Well, we've not found the home port yet." Renfry got to his feet. "Once we set down there—I hadn't intended to say this, but if we ever get to the end of this trip, there's a chance we may get back, providing—" He drummed his fingers against the door casing. "Providing we have more than our share of luck."

"How?" demanded Ashe.

"The controls must now be set with some sort of a guide—perhaps a tape. Once we are grounded and I can get to work, that might just be reversed. But there are a hundred 'ifs' between us and earth, and we can't count on anything."

"There's this, too," Ashe added thoughtfully to that faintest of hopes. "I've been studying the material we have found. If we can crack their language tapes—some of the records we have discovered here must deal with the maintenance and operation of the ship.''

''And where in space are you going to find a Rosetta Stone?'' returned Travis. He did not dare to believe that either of the two discoveries might be possible. ''No common word heritage.''

''Aren't mathematics supposed to be the same, no matter what language? Two and two always add to four, and sums such as that?'' puzzled Ross.

''Please find me some symbols on any of those tapes you've been running through the reader that have the smallest resemblance to any numbers seen on earth.'' Renfry had swung back to the pessimistic side of the balance. ''Anyway—I'm not meddling with the machines in that control cabin while we're still in space.''

Still in space—how long were they going to keep on voyaging? And somehow they found this second lap of their journey into nowhere worse than the first had been. All of them had been secretly convinced that there was only one goal, that their first star port would be their last. But the short pause to refuel now promised a much longer trip. Their only way of telling time was by the hours marked on the dial of Renfry's watch. Days—Ashe made a record of those by counting hours. It was one week since they had left the fuel port—two days more.

Out of the sheer necessity for keeping their minds occupied, they pried at the puzzles offered them in the ship. Ashe had already mastered the operation of a small projector which "read" the wire-kept records, and so opened up not a new world but worlds. The singsong speech which went with the pictures meant nothing to the Terrans. But the pictures—and such pictures! Three-dimensional, colored, they allowed one a window on the incomprehensible life of a complex civilization stretching from star to star.

Races, cultures, and only a third of them humanoid—were these actually factual records? Or were they fiction meant to divert and amuse during the long hours of space travel? Or reports of some service action? They could guess at any answer to what they saw unrolled on the screen of the small machine.

"If this was a police ship and those are authentic reports of past cases," commented Ross, "they sure had their little problems." He had watched with rapt attention a very lurid battle through a jungle which appeared to be largely waterlogged. The enemy there was represented by white amphibious things with a distracting ability to elongate parts of their bodies at will—to the discomfiture of opponents they were so able to ensnare. "On the other hand," he went on, "these may be just cheer-for-the-brave-boys-in-blue story writing to amuse the idle hour. Who are we to know?"

"There's one which I discovered this morning— of more interest to us personally." Ashe sorted through the plate-shaped containers of record wire. "Take a look at this now." He drew out the coil of the jungle battle and inserted the new spool.

Then they saw a sky, gray, lowering with thick

clouds. Below it stretched a waste of what could only be snow such as they knew on their own world. A small party moved into the range of the picture, and the familiar blue suits of those in it were easy to distinguish against the gray-white of the monotonous background.

"Suggest anything to you?" Ashe asked of Ross.

Murdock was leaning forward, studying the picture with a new intentness that argued an unusual interest in so simple a scene.

There were four blue-suited, bald-headed humanoids. They wore no outer clothing and Travis remembered Ross's remarks concerning the insulating qualities of the strange material. Over their heads they did have the bubble helmets, and they were traveling at a pace which suggested the need for caution in footing.

The tape blinked in one of those quick changes to which the viewers had become accustomed. Now they must be surveying the same country from the angle of one of the four blue-clad travelers. There was a sudden, breath-taking drop; the camera must have skimmed at top speed down into a valley. Before them lay a second descent—and the perspectives were out of proportion.

They were not distorted enough, however, to hide what the photographer wanted to record. The viewers were gazing down onto a wide, level space and in that, half buried in banks of drifted snow, was one of the large alien freighters.

"It can't be!" Ross's expression was one of startled surprise.

"Keep watching," Ashe bade.

At a distance, around the stranded half globe, black dots moved. They trailed off on a line marked clearly in the beaten snow as a path which had been worn by a good amount of traffic. There was another disconcerting click and again they saw ice—a huge, murky wall of it, rearing into the gray sky. And directly to that wall of ice led the beaten path.

"The Red time post! It must be! And this ship"—Ross was almost sputtering—"this ship must have been mixed up in that raid on the Reds!"

There was a last click and the screen went blank.

"Where's the rest?" Ross demanded.

"You've seen all there is. If they recorded any more, it's not on this spool." Ashe fingered the colored tag fastened to the container from which he had taken the coil. "Nothing else with a label matching this, either."

"I wonder if the Reds got back at them some way. If that was what killed off the crew later. Germ warfare. . . ." Ross jiggled the switch of the projector back and forth. "I suppose we'll never know."

Then, over their heads, blasting the usual quiet of the ship, came the warning from the control cabin where Renfry kept his self-imposed watch.

"She's triggering for another break-through, fellas. Strap down! I'd say we're due for the big snap very soon!"

They hurried to the bunks. Travis pulled at his protecting webbing. What would they find this time? Another robot-inhabited way stop—or the home port

123

they were longing to reach? He set himself to endure the wrench of the break-through from distance-defeating hyper-space to normal time, hoping that familiarity would render the ordeal easier.

Once more the ship and the men in it were racked by that turnover which defied natural laws and paid in discomfort of mind and body.

"Sun ahead." Travis, opening his eyes, heard Renfry's voice, a little sharpened, through the ship-wide com. "One—two—four planets. We seem to be bound for the second."

More waiting time. Then once more descent into atmosphere, the return of weight, the vibration singing through walls and floors about them. Then the set-down, this time with a slight grating bump, as if the landing had not been so well controlled as it had at the fueling port.

"This is different. . . ." Renfry's report trailed into silence, as if what he saw in the plate had shocked him into speechlessness.

They climbed to the control cabin, crowded below that window on the new world. It must be night—but a night which was alive with reddish light, as if some giant fire filled the sky with the reflection of its fury. And that light rippled even as flames would ripple in their leaping.

"Home?" This time Ross asked the question.

Renfry, entranced as he still watched that display of fiery light, made a usual cautious answer.

"I don't know—I just don't know."

"We'll try a look-see from the port." Ashe took up his planet-side command.

"Might be a volcano," Travis hazarded from his experience in the prehistoric world.

"No, I don't think so. I've only seen one thing like that—"

"I know what you mean." Ross was already on the ladder. "The Northern Lights!"

10

THE CHECKERBOARD spread of the fueling port, different as its architecture had been, was yet not too far removed from their own experience. But this— Travis gazed at the wild display beyond the outer door—this was the most fantastic dream made real.

That flickering red played in tongues along the horizon, filling about a quarter of the sky, ascending in licks up into the heavens. It paled stars and battled the moon which hung there—a moon three times the size of the one which accompanied his home planet.

Rippling out from about the ship was a stretch of cracked, buckled, once-smoothly-surfaced field. There was a faint crackling in the air which did not come from any wind but apparently from static electricity. And the lurid light with its weaving alternately illuminated and reduced to shadow the whole countryside.

"Air's all right." Renfry had cautiously slipped off his helmet. At his report the others freed their own heads. The air was dry, as arid as desert wind.

"Buildings of some sort—in that direction." They turned heads to follow Ross's gesture.

Whereas the towers of the fueling field, ruined as they were, had fingered straightly into the sky, these structures, or structure, hugged the earth, the tallest portion not topping the globe. And nowhere in the red light could Travis sight anything suggesting vegetation. The desolation of the fuel port had been apparent, but here the barrenness was disturbing, almost menacing.

None of them was inclined to go exploring under that fiery sky, and nothing moved in turn toward the ship. If this was another break in their journey, intended for the purpose of servicing their transport, the mechanics had broken down. At last the Terrans withdrew into the ship and closed the port, waiting for day.

"Desert. . . ." Travis said that half to himself but Ashe glanced at him inquiringly.

"You mean—out there?"

"There's a feel in the air," Travis explained. "You learn to recognize it when you've lived most of your life with it."

"Is this the end of the trip?" Ross asked Renfry again.

"I don't know." They had climbed back to the control cabin. Now the technician was standing in front of the main control panel. He was frowning at it. Then he turned suddenly to Travis.

"You feel desert out there. Well, I feel machines—I've lived with them for most of *my* life. We've set down here, there's no indication that we're going to take off again. Nothing but a sense that I have—that we're not finished yet." He laughed, a little self-consciously. "All right, now tell me that I'm seeing ghosts and I'll have to agree."

"On the contrary, I agree with you so thoroughly that I'm not going too far from the ship." Ashe smiled in return. "Do you suppose this is another fuel stop?"

"No robots out," Ross objected.

"Those could have been immobilized or rusted away long ago," Renfry replied. He appeared sorry now that he had raised that doubt.

They went at last to their bunks, but if any of them slept, it was in snatches. To Travis, lying on the soft mattress which fitted itself to the comfort of his body, there was no longer any security—the odd security offered by the ship while in flight. Now outside the shell he could rest his hand against was an unknown territory more liable to offer danger than a welcome. Perhaps the display of fiery lights in the night, perhaps the dry air worked on him to produce the conviction that this was not indeed a world of machines left to carry out tasks set them before his kind had evolved. No, there *was* life here and it waited—outside.

He must have dozed, for it was Ross's hand on his shoulder which brought him awake. And he trailed after the other to the mess. He ate, still silent, but with every nerve in his gaunt body alert, convinced that danger lay outside.

They went armed, strapping on the belts supporting the aliens' blasters. And they issued into a merciless sunlight, as threatening with its white brilliance as the flames of the night before.

Ashe shielded his eyes with his hand. "Try wearing the helmets," he ordered. "They might just cut some of the glare."

He was right. When they fastened down the bubbles, transparent as the material appeared, it cut that daylight so that their eyes were unaffected.

Travis had been right, too, in his belief that they were in desert country. Sand—dunes of white sand, glittering with small sun-reflecting particles which must be blinding to unshielded eyes—crept over the long, deserted landing space. Here were no other grounded ships as they had seen at the first galactic port, only lonely sweeps of sand, unbroken by the faintest hint of vegetation.

Sand—and the buildings, those low, earth-hugging buildings—perhaps a quarter of a mile away.

The four from the ship hesitated at the foot of the ladder. It was not only Renfry's hunch that their voyage was not completed that kept them tied to the globe. The barrenness of the countryside certainly was no invitation to explore. And yet there was always a chance that some discovery might help to solve the abiding riddle of their return.

"We do it this way." Ashe, the veteran explorer,

took over with decisive authority. "You stay here, Renfry—up at the door. Any sign the ship is coming to life again and you fire—on maximum."

A bolt of the force spewed from the narrow muzzle of the alien weapon would produce a crackle of blue fire which should be visible for miles. They were not sure of the range of the helmet coms, but they could be certain of the effectiveness of a force bolt as a warning.

"Can do!" Renfry was already swinging up the ladder, displaying no disappointment in not being one of the explorers.

Then, with Ashe in the center and the lead, the other two flanking him a little behind and to the right and left, the Terrans headed for the buildings. Travis mechanically studied the sand under foot. What he was searching for he could not have told, nor would that loose sand have held tracks—tracks! He glanced back. The faint depressions which marked his footsteps were already almost undistinguishable. There was certainly nothing to indicate that anyone—or *anything*—had passed over that portion of the forgotten base for days, months, years, generations.

But the sand was not everywhere. He stepped aside to avoid a broken block of the pavement tilted up to one side and forming a hollow—a concealing hollow. Travis hesitated, gazing down into that hollow.

Last night a wind had swept across this field; he had felt it up at the port of the ship. Today the air was dead, not a breeze troubled the lightest drift of sand.

And that hollow was free of sand. He did not know why his instincts told him that this was wrong. But because he was nudged by that subconscious uneasiness, he went down on his knees to study the interior of the pocket with the close scrutiny of a hunter-tracker.

So he saw what he might otherwise have missed—that depression marked in the soil where the sand had not drifted. On impulse he rubbed his fingertips hard across that faint mark. There was a greasy feel. He unfastened his helmet long enough to raise those same investigating fingers to his nostrils.

A rank odor—sweat of something alive— something with filthy body habits. He was sure of it! And because that thing must have crouched here for a long time in a well-chosen hiding place from which it could watch the ship undetected, he could also believe it possessed intelligence—of a kind. Snapping down his helmet once more, he reported his find over the com.

"You say it must have been there for some time?" Ashe's voice floated back.

"Yes. And it can't have been gone long either." He was basing all his deductions upon that lingering taint which had been imparted by a warm body to the dusty earth within the small shelter.

"No tracks?"

"They wouldn't show in this stuff." Travis scuffed his foot across a small fan of sand. No, no tracks. But there could only be one place from which the hidden watcher had come—the buildings half concealed by the creeping dunes. He stood up, walked

131

forward, his hand swinging very close to the weapon at his belt. The sense of danger ahead was very strong.

Ashe was before the midpoint of the buildings— there was really only one as they could see now. Its two outlying wings were each connected by a low-lying, windowless passage to the main block. Travis was familiar with the effects of wind and blown-sand erosion upon rock outcrops. Here the same factors had been in operation to pit surfaces, round and polish away corners and edges, until the walls were like the dunes rising about them.

There were no windows—no visible doorways. But at the end of the wing before Travis there was a dip in a sand dune, breaking the natural line chiseled by the wind. It was a break unusual enough to catch his alerted attention.

"Over here," he called softly, forgetting that the helmet com and not the air waves carried his voice. Slowly, with the caution of a stalker after wary game, he moved toward that break in the dune. There were no tracks, yet he was almost certain that the disturbance had been recent and made by the passage of something moving with a purpose—not just the result of a vagary of the night wind.

He rounded the pointing finger of one dune which now arose at his shoulder height against the wall, and knew he was right. The sand had obviously been thrust back—blocked loosely on either side—as if some door had opened outward from the building, pushing the sand drift before it.

"Cover him!" Ashe's shadow crossed the sun-drenched sand of the dune, met the other one cast by Ross. With the two time agents at his back, the Apache began a detailed inspection of that length of wall.

Although his eyes could detect no difference in that surface, his fingers did when he ran them along about waist level. There was a strip here, extending down to the ground, which was not of the same texture as the substance above and to the sides. But though he pressed, pulled, and applied his weight to move it in every way he could think to try, there was no yielding. He was sure that that portion could open, to cause the marks in the sand.

At last, getting down on his hands and knees, Travis crawled along, trying to force fingertips under at ground's edge. And so he discovered a harsh turf of hair protruding. Combined efforts of knife tip and fingers worked the wisp loose. It was coarse stuff, coarser than any animal's he had ever seen, each separate hair enlarged to the size of half a dozen normal Terran specimens. And it was a gray-white in color, melting into the shade of the sand so it could not be distinguished against the dunes.

Having a greasy feel it clung to Travis' fingers, and he did not really need the evidence of his nose to tell him that it was rankly odorous. He brought it back to Ashe, his distaste in handling it growing steadily. The latter put the trophy away in one of his belt pockets.

"Any chance of opening that?" Ashe indicated the hidden door in the wall.

"Not that I can see," Travis returned. "It is probably secured on the inside."

They studied the building dubiously. Behind its length, as far as they could judge, there was only a waste of sand dunes reaching out and out to the sky rim where the fire had played the night before. If there was any riddle to be solved, its answer lay inside this locked box and not in the desert countryside.

"Ross, you stay here. Travis, move on to the end of the wing. Stay there where you can see Ross—and me, as I go along the back."

Ashe used the same care as the Apache had done, running his hands along the eroded surface, seeking any indication of another door which might possibly be forced. He went the entire length of the building and came back—with nothing to report.

"There were windows once and a door. But they were all walled up a long time ago, sealed tight now. We might pick out the sealing, given time and the right tools."

Ross's voice came through the helmet coms. "Any chance of getting in through the roof, chief?"

"If you're game to try—up with you!"

Travis stood against the wall which refused to give up its secrets and Ross used him as a ladder, mounting to the roof. He moved inward and the two left on the ground lost sight of him. But on Ashe's orders he made a running commentary of what he saw through the com.

"Not much sand—you'd think there would be more. . . . Hulloo!" There was an eagerness in that sudden exclamation. "This *is* something! Round plates set in circles all over—about the size of quarters. They are solid and you can't move them."

"Metal?" Ashe asked.

"Nooo . . ." the reply was hesitant. "Seem more like some kind of glass, only they aren't transparent."

"Windows?" suggested Travis.

"Too small," Ross protested. "But there are a lot of them—all over. Wait!" The urgency in that last cry alerted both the men on the ground. "Red—they're turning red!"

"Get out of there! Jump!" Ashe's order barked loudly in all their helmets.

Ross obeyed without question, landing with a paratrooper's practiced roll on one of the dune crests. The others scrambled to join him, all their attention focused on the roof of the sealed building. Perhaps something in the sun-repelling qualities of their helmets enabled them to see those rays as faint reddish lines cutting up from the roof into the reach of the sky.

The skin on Travis' bare hands tingled with a pins-and-needles sensation as if the circulation in it had been arrested and was not coming back to duty. Ross scrambled up out of the sand and shook himself vigorously.

"What in the world is going on?" There was an unusual note of awe in his tone.

"I think—some fireworks to discourage you. I believe that we may assume whoever lives in there is definitely not at home to curious callers. Not only that, but the householder has some mighty unpleasant gadgets to back up his desire for privacy. Probably just as well we didn't find his, her, or its front door unlocked.''

Travis could no longer see those thin fiery lines. Either the power had been shut off, or the rays were now past the point of detection by human eyes, even with the aid of the helmet. That coarse hair, the repulsive odor—and now this. Somehow the few facts did not add properly. The hair, of course, could have been left by a watchdog, or the equivalent on this particular planet of a watchdog. That supposition would also fit with the low entrance into the building. But a watchdog that kept to carefully chosen cover, the best in the whole landscape, and stayed to spy, maybe for hours, on the ship—? Those facts did not fit with the general nature of any animal he had ever known. Rather, that action matched with intelligence, and intelligence meant man.

"I believe they are nocturnal," Ashe said suddenly. "That fits with all we've seen so far. This sun glare may be as painful for them as it is for us without helmets. But at night—"

"Going to sit up and watch what happens?" Ross asked.

"Not out in the open. Not until we know more."

Silently Travis agreed to that. There was a furtiveness about the last night's spying which made him wary. And to his mind this world was far more frightening and sinister than the fueling port. Its very arid barrenness held a nebulous threat he had never sensed in the desert lands of his own planet.

They walked back to the ship, climbed the ladder, and were glad to close the port upon the dead white glare, to unhelm in the blue glow of the interior.

"What did you see?" Ashe asked Renfry.

"Murdock taking a high dive from the roof and then some red lines, very faint, shooting up from all over its surface. What did you do, push the wrong doorbell?"

"Probably waked somebody up. I don't think that's a very healthy place to go visiting. Lord—what a stink!" Ross ended, sniffing.

Ashe held on his palm the tuft of hair and the odor rising from it was not only noticeable in the usual scentless atmosphere of the ship, but penetrating in its foulness.

They carried the lock into the small cubbyhole which might once have been the quarters of the commander and where Ashe had assembled his materials for study. In spite of the noisome effluvia of their trophy, they gathered around as he pulled the tuft apart hair by hair and spread it flat.

"Those hairs—so thick!" Renfry marveled.

"If they *are* hairs. What I wouldn't give for a lab!" Ashe placed a clear sheet of the aliens' writing materials to imprison the lock.

"That smell—" Travis, remembering how he had handled the noisome find, rubbed his hand back and forth across his thigh.

"Yes?" Ashe prompted.

"Well—I think that comes from just plain filthiness, sir. Or, part might be because the hairs are from a creature we don't know."

"Alien metabolism." Ashe nodded. "Each Terran race has a distinctive body odor far more apparent to a man of another than to one of his own breed. But what are you getting at, Travis?"

"Well, if that does come from some—some man" he used the term because he had no other—"and not from an animal, then I'd say he was living in a regular sty. And that means either a pretty low type of primitive, or a degenerate."

"Not necessarily," Ashe pointed out. "Bathing entails water, and we haven't seen any store of water here."

"Sure, there's no water we can see. But they must have some. And I think—" Only there were few proofs he could offer to bolster his argument.

"Might be. Anyway, tonight we'll watch and see what *does* come out of the booby-trapped box over there."

They napped during the day, Renfry in the control cabin as usual. None of them could see any reason why the ship had earthed on this sand pile, and the very barrenness of the place reinforced Renfry's belief that this could not be their ultimate goal. It was only logic that the ship must have originally voyaged from some center of civilization—and this was not that.

The glare of the sun was gone and dusk clothed the mounds of creeping sand when they gathered again at the door in the outer skin to watch the building and the stretch of ground lying between them and that enigmatic block.

"How long do you suppose we'll have to wait?" Ross shifted position.

"No time at all," Ashe answered softly. "Look!"

From behind the dune which marked the low doorway Travis had discovered, there showed a very faint reddish glow.

11

HAD THE flaming display of the late evening before been in progress, they could not have spotted that. And now, in the dusk, with the shapes of the dunes distorting vision, it was difficult to see. Ashe was counting slowly under his breath. As he reached "twenty" the glow vanished with a sudden completeness which suggested the slamming of a door.

Travis strained his eyes, watching the end of that masking dune. If the thing which had spied upon them the night before was coming back to the old position, the shortest route to take would cross that point. But he had seen nothing so far.

There was a very thin sound, but that came from the opposite direction, a whispering from the open country. Then a pat of arid air touched his cheek, wind rising with the coming of night. And the whispering must be the moving of sand grains under its first tentative stir.

"We could ambush one scout," Ross observed wistfully.

"Their senses may be more acute than ours. Certainly if they are nocturnal, their night sight will be. And we can believe that they are already suspicious of us. Also, I'd like to know a little more about the nature of something or someone I'm going to lay a trap for."

Travis only half heard Ashe. Surely he had seen a flicker of movement out there. Yes! His fingers closed on the older man's arm in swift warning pressure. A blob of shadow had slipped from the end of the dune, skidded quickly into hiding, heading straight for the hollow behind the upended block of masonry. Was the spy now settled in for a long spell of duty in that improvised observation post? Or tonight would he, she or it venture closer to the ship?

The dusk deepened and with the coming of true dark the tongues of fire danced in the sky. Though the light afforded by that display was not steady, it did illuminate the smoother ground immediately about the globe. Any attack on the part of the unknown natives could be sighted by the men on guard above. The Terrans knew, though, that with the ladder up and open port some dozen feet removed from ground level they had little to fear from any actual attempt to force their stronghold. Unless the creatures out there possessed weapons able to cut down the distance advantage.

"Close the inner-lock door," Ashe said suddenly.

"We'll shut off the ship's light, make it hard for them to spot us here."

With the lock shut and the blue light of the ship blanked out, they lay flat on the floor of the cramped space, trying not to hamper each other, awaiting the next move on the part of the lurker or lurkers below.

"Something there," Ross warned softly. "To the left—right at the end of that last dune."

The lurker was impatient. A blob of dark, which might have been a head, moved against the white sand. Wind sang around the ship, gathering up grit. The men snapped down their helmets in protection against that. But those whirls of sand devils did not appear to bother the native.

"I think there are more than one of them," Travis said. "That last movement came too far away from the first I sighted."

"Could they be getting ready to rush us?" Ross wondered.

Oddly enough, none of the Terrans had drawn his blasters. The perch was so high above the surface over which the attackers must advance, and the smooth rounding of the unclimbable globe was so apparent, that both gave them a sense of security.

The dark thing made a dart toward the globe. And it either ran bent almost double—or else on all fours! One of the startling jumps of the sky's light spot-lighted the form, and the watchers exclaimed.

Man or animal? The thing had four long limbs, and two more projections at mid-body. The head was round, down-held as it darted, so that they could not sight any features. But the whole body was matted with hair—dark hair, not light to match the tuft Travis had found. There was no sign of clothing, nor did the creature appear to be carrying weapons.

For a single moment that flitting shadow paused, facing the ship. Then it scurried back into hiding among the dunes once more. There was another flash of movement which the watchers could hardly detect, as this time the body of the runner merged in color with the sand about it.

"That might have been your hair shedder," remarked Ashe. "It certainly was lighter in color than the first one."

"They come in different colors—but all about the same size," Ross added. "And what in the world are they?"

"Nothing in our world." Ashe was definite about that. "We can believe, though, that they are interested in this ship and that they are trying to find some way of getting to it undetected."

"The way they move," Travis said, "as if they feared attack. . . . They must have enemies."

"Enemies to be associated with such a ship as this?" Ashe jumped to the point with his usual speed of understanding. "Yes, that could be. Only I don't believe that there has been a ship here for a long, long time."

"Memories passed down—"

"Memories would mean they are men!" Travis was not aware until he voiced those words out of a sense of outrage that he abhorred association with those half-seen creatures in the dunes.

"To themselves they may be men," Ashe returned, "and we might represent monsters. All relative, son. At any rate, I believe that they do not regard us with kindness."

"What I wouldn't give for a flashlight now," Ross said wistfully. "I'd like to catch one of them in a beam for a really good look."

They were treated to a wealth of half glimpses of the natives moving through the sand hills as the minutes crawled on, but never did they have a chance really to study one.

"I think they're working their way around to come in behind the globe—on our blind side," Travis offered, having traced at least two in that possible direction.

"Won't do them any good—this is the only opening." Ross sounded close to smug.

But the thought of the natives coming in behind the globe could not be accepted so easily by Travis. Every buried instinct of hunter and desert warrior argued that such a chance threatened his own security. Reason told him, though, that there was only this one door to the ship, and that it was easily defended. They need only close it and nothing could reach them.

"What was the reason for this port anyway?" Ross pursued the big question a few seconds later. "There must have been some purpose for stopping here. Do we have to find something—or do something—before we can leave again?"

That thought had ridden all their minds, but Ross had brought fear into the open. And what if the solution lay over there, in that building to which there was no entrance—unless one could be forced at night? A nighttime entrance guarded by the flitting hairy things which could see in the dark and whose home hunting-ground it was. . . .

"The building—?" Travis made a question of it. He felt Ashe stir beside him.

"Might just be," the other assented. "If we are hung up here much longer, we can try burning our way in by day. These blasters pack a pretty hefty charge when set at maximum."

Travis' hand shot out, clamped down on Ashe's shoulder. His helmet was locked against the grit drift in the wind, but his hand had been resting on the edge of the door casing and had caught that thud-thud transmitted by the outer skin of the globe. Below the bulge which kept the Terrans from viewing the ground directly under the curve of the side, something was beating on the metallic outer casing of the vessel—for what purpose and with what result, he could not guess. He groped for Ashe's hand, drew it out beside his own and pressed the palm flat to get the same message.

"Pounding, I think." He realized that the messages in helmet coms could not reach the ears of lurkers below. "But why?"

"Trying to hole the ship?" Ross hung over the other two. "They've no chance of getting through the hull—or have they?" His concluding flash of anxiety was shared by the rest. What did they know of the resources of the natives?

Coiled beside Travis was the ladder. Dare he push that out, climb over to see what the night creepers were doing below? The thud of the pounding appeared to him to be taking on both speed and intensity. Suppose by some miracle, or the use of some unknown tool, the hairy things could pierce the outer skin of the globe? Then there would be no possible hope of escape from this forgotten desert.

He began to edge the ladder forward. Ashe made a grab which the younger man fended away.

"We have to see," he said, "we *have* to!"

Ross and Ashe moved together and in that narrow space blocked each other long enough for Travis to squeeze through the door, swing over the lip and climb down the length of his own body. Then he felt the ladder catch tight and knew that the other two were preventing its descent to ground level.

Gripping the rungs tightly, holding his body as close as he could to the surface of the ship, Travis looked down. The play of red flashes against the sky furnished a weird light for the activity below, for there *was* activity. He had been right. The hairy things had crept in unseen from behind the ship, and a group of them were now clustered about the base of the globe. But what they were doing he could not make out in the constant flickering of the light. Then one reared from its usual quadrupedal stance, and raised its forearms over its hump of head. The appendages at its midsection gave a twitch, writhed out in a manner which suggested bonelessness, and clasped tight to the ship.

The creature gave a bound into the air and then hung, its hind feet now a foot or so off the ground. Apparently it held on by the grip of waist tentacles against the globe, while the fists or paws on its forelimbs pounded vigorously against that surface. There was something about that hitching climb, for it gave another squirm upward as Travis watched, which spelled for him a purposeful malignancy.

Now a second creature had hitched itself by mid-section tentacles to the hull and was beginning to ascend. Travis could sight no weapons, nothing but those steadily pounding fists. But neither did he have any wish to battle the slow climbers. He reported to Ashe and was ordered back into the ship. They closed the port, took the precaution of sealing it as if making ready for flight, and then loosened their helmets.

Neither the pounding nor the sound of the climbers could reach them now. But Travis did not believe that the creatures had ceased their efforts to win into the ship, futile as those efforts might seem. The Terrans climbed to the control cabin to watch the outer world on the limited view of the vision plate. Renfry looked puzzled.

"I don't get it. I still say that I'm sure this isn't the end of the flight. But I can't tell you why, or the why of this port, either. If the answer lies in that building, you'll have to crack it open. But we may have a better cracker than just those hand blasters."

Ross caught his meaning first. "The ship's guns!"

"Might be."

"*Can* we use them?" Ashe wanted to know.

"Well, they're less a top secret than the rest of the stuff around here. Remember this?" He pressed a lever. Lights winked, that word from a vanished language spoke out of the thin air. It was all as it had been on their exploration of the ship.

"And you can fire them?"

"The chief—my chief—doped out that this does that"—Renfry fingered another switch he did not depress. "As far as I deduce, one of those king-sized blasters should just about clip across the roof of your strongbox. We can try it on for size any time you're ready."

But Ashe was rubbing his jaw in that absent-minded way which meant he had not yet come to a decision. "Too much guessing in all of this. We don't know that we have to crack that place open in order to lift ship again. In fact, if we did crack it and couldn't find what we needed—we wouldn't be any better off. These natives must depend upon that shelter for their lives. Break it open and they're just as dead as if we mowed them down with blasters. They may not be anything or anybody we'd care to live with, but this is their world and we're intruders. I'd like to wait a little before I try anything as drastic as blowing up the place."

None of them was inclined to push him into action. Outside the flames beat into the night sky, and the white of the moon they had noted the night before was marred by a more yellow gleam from a smaller satellite trailing behind the larger. But of the activity of the dune skulkers the screen gave them no clue.

That came not by sight but by a startling shifting of the ship itself. How had the creatures outside achieved that movement? Perhaps, Travis imagined, by the sheer weight of many creeping bodies plastered to the hull. The globe canted from its landing position. And maybe that triggered the flying controls. For the now-familiar warnings of a take-off alerted them all.

"No!" Renfry protested, "we can't—not yet—not until we know why."

But the engines the Terrans did not understand, and could not hope to control, had no ears for that feeble defiance. Perhaps only a time limit had governed their visit, a full day and night of planetary time. Or maybe it was the strange attack of the hairy things.

And those creatures—would they free themselves in time, drop to the ground as the ship lifted, warned by the vibration? Or would they cling in stupid concentration upon their attack, to be carried out into the freezing blackness of the eternal space night?

The unwilling crew of the ship followed the old routine of strap down and wait for the wrench of blast-off, the break into hyper-space. Again they were being carried into the unknown with perhaps a long voyage ahead.

But it was not to be the same this time. Travis noticed the first departure from the usual routine. The take-off was not so severe—or else he had adjusted to it far better than he ever had before. He did not black out completely, nor did he have to undergo that terrible twisting. And he heard Renfry's voice exclaim in wonder:

"I don't think we went into hyper! What happened?"

They were up and about, watching the vision plate of the ship. Renfry's guess was right. For instead of the complete blankness which closed in upon them when they made a big inter-system jump, they saw now the receding orb of the desert planet, its face a mass of shifting color as they withdrew from it.

"Must be heading for another planet in this same system," Ashe supplied one answer. And, as the hours wore on, they believed that was the right one. The ship now appeared to be on course for the third planet of that unknown sun.

"Do we visit them all?" inquired Ross with some of his old flippancy. "If so—why? Milk delivery?"

Three days went by, four. They ate the alien food and moved restlessly about the ship, unable to pay attention for any length of time to anything but the screen in the control cabin. Then on the sixth day, came the signals of an approaching landing.

On the vision plate the goal showed a vivid blue-green, patched here and there with orange-red. It was arresting in its splashes of contrasting color. They had drawn lots for the occupancy of the three seats in the control cabin, and the odd man to be relegated to the bunk below. So Travis now lay alone and unseeing in the heart of the throbbing globe, wondering what new future they must confront.

The ship set down this time in the planet's day. The Apache freed himself from his straps, stumbled in the return clutch of gravity to the ladder and climbed up to share the others' view of the new world.

"No—!"

The ruined towers standing starkly to portion off the expanse of the fueling port had speared as straightly into the sky—but they had not been like this one. Against a background of cloudless, delicate pink, was an opaline dome, curved in flowing lines which spiraled up in turn to a fragile, frosting lace. It was impossible to believe that this was the result of man's construction.

Torn lace . . . . As he studied those lifting spans, Travis could mark the breaks which spoiled the perfect pattern. Yet in spite of that damage there was still the fantastic beauty of foam and light and play of rainbow color. It rose out of dark foliage with a tinge of blue which was not a part of the green of his own world's leaves.

And those leafy branches stirred almost languidly as if light breezes pulled at them, showing here and there a touch of other colors. Fruit? Flowers?

Renfry brought their attention away from the scene which was so ethereal as to seem unreal.

"Look!"

He was on his feet before the main control board, his hands grasping the back of the pilot's seat so tightly that the muscles stood out on his taut arms. For the board had taken on life. They had witnessed the flickers of light which had heralded the readying of the ship's guns. This was something else—a line of small winks of brilliance flowing unevenly down the rows of levers and buttons. And where each flashed a lever arose, a button sank or snapped above the level of the board. There was a final burst of light from a spot Travis could have covered with his thumb. And there a lid opened, a cavity beneath disgorged a small, coin-shaped bit of red metal which tinkled out, to roll across the floor.

Renfry came to life, dove to catch it up. He held it in his hand as if the disk was something very precious indeed.

"Home port!" He swung about to face them, his eagerness lighting a flame in his eyes. "This is the home port! And I think I am holding the course tape!"

There could be no other explanation for what they had just witnessed. The journey plotted by a dying man had come to its full conclusion. That small button of metal Renfry had closed fist upon, held now not only the secret of their arrival—but of their return. If they were ever to regain their own world, it would be because they had solved the workings of that disk.

Yet Travis' eyes went from the technician's clenched hand and what it held, back to the vision plate. The picture there was of a gentle wind lifting flowering branches about a tower of opal against a sky of palest rose. And the immediate future seemed at that moment more entrancing than the more distant one.

Perhaps Ashe shared that feeling at the moment. For the senior time agent moved toward the inner ladder. He paused at the well and looked back over his shoulder, to say with a strange simplicity:

"Let us go out—now."

12

IF THERE had once been a wide landing strip here, the
space was long since swallowed by a cover of green.
From the mass crushed by the landing of the ship
came the scent of growing things, some spicy, some
rank.

The Terrans had not worn their helmets, nor did
they need to here. A sunlight no stronger than that of
early summer in the temperate zone of their own
world greeted them. And there was no burden of
sand in the soft wind which whirled flower petals and
torn leaves from the wreckage under their feet.

Now that they had a wider view than that offered
by the vision plate, they noted other breaks in the
luxuriance of growing things. The opal tower with
its fantastic form was flanked by another building as
strange and as far removed from the style of its

companion as the desert world was from this green one. For the massive blocks of dull red, geometric in their solidity, could not have sprung from the same creative imagination—or perhaps from even the same race or age.

And beyond that was another, with knife-sharp gables and narrow windows secretive in its gray walls. It had a pointed roof of some rough material, dull under the sun, and gave rootage in places to vines, even a small tree. But again it was not of the same vintage as the fairylike dome or the massive blocks.

"Why—?" Ross's head turned slowly as he looked from one of those totally dissimilar buildings to the next. All were tall, dwarfing the globe, and all had their lower stories hidden by the vegetation.

Travis thought back to a past which seemed a little blurred by all which had happened lately. There were places on his own world where a Zuñi village in miniature stood beside a Sioux lodge or an Apache wickiup.

"A museum?" He ventured the only explanation he could see.

Ashe's face was pale under his fading tan. He stared raptly from dome to block, block to sharply accented gables. "Or else a capital where each embassy built in their home style."

"And now it is all dead," Travis added. For that was true. This was as deserted as the fueling port.

"Capital perhaps—of a galactic empire. What there is to be learned here! A treasure house—" Ashe was breathing fast. "We may have the treasures of a thousand worlds to uncover here."

"And who will ever know—or care?" Ross asked. "Not that I'm not ready to go and look for them."

Travis tensed. There was a stirring in the mass of tangled vegetation where the grounding of the globe had flattened some of the fern trees, bearing with them others tied together by vines. He watched that shaking of bruised and broken branches. Something alive was working its way from a point about a hundred yards away from the ship toward the wall of still-standing plants, its progress marked by that movement. And the fugitive thing must be fairly large by the amount of displacement.

Had that crawling unseen thing been injured in the crash of the tree ferns? Was it now dragging itself off to die? Travis listened, striving to hear more than the rustling of the leaves. But if the thing was hurt, it made no complaint. Animal? Or—something else? Something as alien as the dune lurkers, more than animal, yet different from man as they knew man?

"It's in cover now," breathed Ross. "Couldn't have been too hurt or it wouldn't have moved so lively."

"I think we can believe that this world isn't as empty as it might look to the first glance," Ashe said a little dryly. "And what about those?"

"Those" came lightly, drifting across the torn clearing caused by the descent of the globe. They flapped gossamer wings once or twice to keep airborne, but their attention was manifestly centered on the ship.

And what were they? Birds? Insects? Flying

155

mammals? Travis could almost believe the four small creatures were a weird combination of all three species. Their long narrow wings, prismatic and close to transparent, resembled those of an insect. Yet they had bodies equipped with three legs, two smaller ones in front ending in three clawshaped digits, one larger limb in back with even more pronounced talons. Their heads seemed to be set directly on their shoulders with no visible neck and were round at the top, narrowing to a curved beak, while their eyes—four of them!—protruded on short stalks, two in front and two in back. And their triangles of bodies were clothed in plushy fur of a pale and frosted blue.

Slowly, in a solemn, silent procession, they drifted toward the ship. The second in line broke out of formation, dipping groundward. Its hind claws found anchorage on a stub of broken branch and its wings folded together above its back as might those of a Terran butterfly.

The two last in line flapped back and forth across the open port twice and then wheeled, flew off, mounting into the sky to clear the treetops. But the leader came on, until it hung, beating wings now and then to maintain altitude, directly before the entrance of the ship.

It was impossible to read any expression in those stalked eyes, a brilliant blue. But none of the four Terrans felt any repulsion or alarm as they had upon their encounter with the nocturnal desert people. Whatever the flyer was, they could not believe that it was either aggressive or a possible danger to them.

156

Renfry expressed their common reaction to the creature first:

"Funny little beggar, isn't he? Like to see him closer. If they're all the same as him here, we don't have to worry."

Why the technician should refer to the winged thing as "he" was obscure. But the creature was attractive enough to hold their concentrated interest. Ross snapped his fingers and held out his hand in welcome.

"Here, boy," he coaxed.

Those brilliant bits of blue winked as the eye stalks moved, the wings beat, and the flyer approached the port. But not close enough for the Terrans to touch. It hung there, suspended in mid-air for a long moment. Then with a flurry of beating wings, sparking rainbows, it mounted skyward, its partner taking off from the brush below at the same moment to join it. A few seconds later they vanished as if they had never been.

"Do you suppose it is intelligent?" Ross watched after the vanished flyer, his disappointment mirrored on his usually impassive face.

"Your guess is as good as mine," Ashe replied. "Renfry," he spoke to the technician, "you have your journey tape now. Can you reset it?"

"I don't know. Wish I had a manual—at least some type of guide. Do you suppose you can find such a thing here?"

"Why are you in such a big hurry to leave, chief? We only got here and it looks like a pretty good vacation spot to me." Ross raised his head a little to eye the dome where opal lights played under the sun's rays.

"That is just why," Ashe replied quietly. "There are too many temptations here."

Travis understood. To Ashe the appeal of those waiting buildings, of the knowledge which they might contain, must be almost overpowering. They could postpone work on the ship, delay and delay, fascinated by this world and its secrets. He knew the same pull, though perhaps in a lesser degree. Before it trapped them all, they must struggle against that enveloping desire to plunge into the green jungle, slash a path to the opal dome and see for themselves what wonders it housed.

Ashe was sorely tempted. And because he was the man he was, he must be fighting that temptation now, believing that if he once plunged wholeheartedly into exploration, he might not be able to stop. Also Renfry was offering them an excuse to do just that by wishing for some aid in the problem of the tape.

An hour later the three of them did leave the ship, Renfry remaining in charge there. Using the lowest beam of the blasters, they cut a path into the woods. Travis picked up a flower head. Five wide petals, fluted, crinkled a little at the tips, were a deep cream in color, shading orange at the heart. Resting on his palm, those petals began to move visibly, closing until he held a bud instead of a flower. He could not toss away the blossom. Its color was too arresting, its spicy scent appealing. He worked the short stem into one of the latches of a belt pouch, where, the heat of his hand removed, the flower opened once again.

Nor did it fade or droop in spite of the shortness of its stem.

Now, out of the direct rays of the sun, the Terrans found the air cool, moist, heavy with the odor of too luxuriant vegetation. Not that those odors were unpleasant—in fact, they were overpoweringly good. Spicy scents warred with perfumes and the sharper smell of earth as their feet scuffed through the mass of dead leaves.

"Whew!" Ross waved his hand back and forth in front of his face as if to set up a reviving current of air. "Perfume factory—or what have you! I feel as if I were burrowing through about a ton of roses!"

Ashe appeared to have lost some of his somberness since they had left the ship. "With another of carnations thrown in," he agreed. "I think I can detect"—he sniffed and then sneezed— "some cloves and maybe a few nutmegs into the bargain."

Travis breathed shallowly. He had welcomed the mixture of perfumes minutes earlier. Now he found himself wishing instead to face a wind with a burden of sage and piñon in place of these cloying scents in their thick abundance.

The jungle grew clear up to the base of the opaline building. And the structure itself loomed far higher from ground level than had appeared true from the port of the ship. They worked their way along, hunting the entrance which must exist somewhere, unless the inhabitants had all worn wings. Oddly enough—though there were windows in plenty of stories above, many opening on small airy balconies—the first story showed no openings at all. Here were panels set in carved frames alternating with solid blocks of the opal material. And each panel was patterned in a gleaming mosaic, not forming any recognized design but merely wedding color to color in blending shades.

The Terrans cut their way through underbrush and reached the end of the wall. This was a large building occupying the space of a normal Terran city block. But around the corner they found the door, at the head of a curling ramp. The portal extended almost the full height of the first story and it was open, a carved archway. The frame was like frozen lace, with here a curve and there a point cracked and gone.

They hesitated. Save for the sighing of the wind, the sound of leaf against moving leaf, and some small twitters and squeaks from the unseen inhabitants of the green world which lay about the foot of the ramp, there was quiet—the quiet of the forgotten.

Ashe stepped onto the ramp, his soft-shod feet making not the slightest whisper. He climbed the gentle slope almost reluctantly, as if he did not really want to know what waited within.

Travis and Ross came behind. There were pockets of dead leaves caught in the curves of the ramp, and more drifted inside the open portal. They shuffled through them, to come into a hall which was breathtaking in its height. For it went up and up, until they were dizzied when they tried to follow its inner spiral with their eyes. And covering this expanse was the great opaline dome. The sunlight shone through it, painting rainbows on walls and on the ramp which climbed in a coil along the walls, serving other archways of fetter-lace on every floor level.

Here there was none of the brilliance of the outside mosaics. The spread of color was sharply reduced to soft, faded shades, a dusky violet, a pallid green, a dusty rose, a cream. . . .

" . . . forty-eight—forty-nine—fifty! Fifty doors up and down that ramp at least." Ross kept his voice to a murmur and yet that echo of a whisper carried eerily back to them. "Where do we start?" Now his tone was definitely higher, in challenge to that echo and the stillness which deadened it.

Ashe left them, crossed the expanse of hall, both of his hands going out to a niche. When they hurried after him they discovered he was holding a small statuette carved of a dusky violet stone. Like the blue flyers, the subject bore baffling resemblances to living things they knew, and yet was in its totality alien.

"Man?" Ross wondered. "Animal?"

"Totem? God?" Travis added out of his own knowledge and background.

"All or any," conceded Ashe. "But it is a work of art."

That they could all recognize, even if the subject still puzzled them. The figure was posed erect on two slender hind limbs, both of which terminated in feet of long, narrow, widely separated, clawed digits. The body, also slender but with a well-defined waist and broad shoulders, was closer to the human in general appearance, and there were two arms held aloft, as if the creature was about to leap outward into space. But it would have a better chance of survival in such a leap than those now passing the statuette from hand to hand. From the arms supported skin wing-flaps, extended on ribs not unlike those possessed by the Terran bats.

The head was the least human, almost grotesque in its ugliness to the time agents' eyes. There were sharply pointed ears, overshadowing in their size and extension the rest of the features which were crowded together in the forepart of the face. Eyes were set deep within cavities under heavy skull ridges, the nose was simply a vertical slit above a mouth from which thin vestiges of lips curled back to display a usable and frightening set of fangs. And yet its ugliness was not repulsive, not horrifying. There was no clothing to suggest that it represented an intelligent being. Yet all of them were certain, the longer they examined the figure, that it had not been meant to portray an animal.

To the touch the violet stone was smooth and cool, and when Travis held it out into a patch of light from the dome, the statuette sparkled as might a gem. The careful detail of the figure was in contrast to the abstraction of the murals on the outer walls, more akin to the carvings on the dome and about the doorways.

Ross drew his finger along the interior of the niche where Ashe had found the image. Dust piled there was pushed out to the floor. How long had the winged one stood there undisturbed?

Ashe carried it in the crook of his arm as they went on—not up the spiral of the ramp but into the first of the open doorways on ground level. But the room beyond was empty, lighted through slits high on the wall. They wandered on. More empty rooms, no trace of those who had once lived here—if this had been a dwelling place and not a building of public use. It was as if the inhabitants when they had at last withdrawn, had stripped it bare, forgetting only the little statue in the hall.

As they came from the last bare chamber, Ross sighed and leaned against the wall.

"I don't know how you feel about it," he announced. "But I've swallowed more than my share of dust this past hour or so. Also breakfast was a long time back. A coffee break right about now—providing we had the coffee—might be heartening."

They didn't have coffee, but they had come provided with the foam drink from the ship. So, sitting in a row across the ramp, they sucked in turn from containers of that and ate some of the "corn" cakes they carried for trail rations.

"Be good to have some fresh food," Travis said wistfully. The rather monotonous diet from the ship's stores satisfied hunger but did not appeal to his taste. He allowed himself the luxury of visualizing a sizzling steak and all that would accompany it back at the ranch.

"Maybe some on the hoof—out there." Ross, his hands full, pointed with his chain toward the riot of greenery they could sight from their present perch. "We could go hunting. . . ."

"How about that?" Travis roused and turned to Ashe eagerly. "Dare we try?"

But the older agent did not warm to the suggestion. "I wouldn't kill—until I knew what I was killing."

For a moment Travis did not understand, and then the meaning of the rather ambiguous statement sank in. How could they be sure that the prey was not—man! Or man's equivalent here? But he still wanted that steak, with a longing which gnawed at him.

"Do we climb?" Ross stood up. "This'll be an all-day job right here, if we stick to it. I'd say the cupboard's bare, though."

"Maybe." Ashe cradled his bat-thing in his arm. "We can take a quick look through the ground floor of that big red block to the north."

They fought their way through the thick wall of brush, grass, tree and vine to the red building of the monolithic architecture. Here again they faced an open door, this one narrow as the window slits, as if grudging any entrance at all.

"I'd say the guys who built this one didn't like their neighbors too well," Ross commented. "This could make a pretty good fort if you had to have one. That domed place is wide open."

"Different peoples. . . ." Travis had been a little in advance, lingering for a moment before he took the step which would bring him over the threshold. Once inside he froze.

"Trouble!" His blaster was out, ready to fire.

There was a wide hall before him, as there had been in the dome building. But where that had been clean and bare, this one was different.

A series of partitions some five or six feet high cut back and forth, chopping the floor space into a crazy quilt of oddly shaped and sized spaces, with little chance to see from one to the next. But that did not bother Travis so much as the message recorded by his nose.

The odor of the night creatures had been something like this. It was the taint of a lair—a lair long in use. It smelled of decay, alien body reek, dried and rotted vegetation and animal matter. Something denned here, used this place freely for some time.

It was the eagerness of that strange hunter which betrayed it. A low, throaty murmur, such as a cat might utter when intent upon unsuspecting prey, carried across the shadows.

Travis spun around. He saw the hunched shape balancing on top of a partition, knew it was about to launch straight for him. And he pressed the firing button of the blaster as he brought it up.

The attacker was caught in mid-air. A terrible yowl of rage, and pain, echoed and re-echoed about the massive walls. A flailing limb, well provided with claws, raked across Travis' body from the waist down, sending him reeling from the door into the greater gloom. Just then Ross and Ashe burst in, to center the full beams of their weapons on the rolling, caterwauling thing making a second attempt at Travis.

Whatever it was, the creature possessed abnormal vitality. It was not until those blast rays met and crossed in its body that it lay still. Travis scrambled to his feet, shaken. He knew that if he had not had that split second of warning, he would be dead—or so badly mauled he would have longed for death.

He limped back toward the door, his thigh and leg feeling numb from the force of that smashing stroke. But under his questing hand the fabric of the suit was untorn, and there seemed to be no open wound.

"Did it get you?" Ashe came to meet him, pushing aside his hands to look at his body. Travis, still shaken, winced under the exploring probe of the other's fingers.

"Just bruised. What was it?"

Ross arose from a gingerly inspection of the remains. "After the blasting we gave it, your guess is as good as mine. But it is sure sudden death on six legs—and that's no overstatement."

The blasters had not left too much to identify, that was true. But the thing had been six-legged, furred, and carnivorous—and it was about eight feet long with fangs and claws in proportion to the size.

"Sabertooth, local variety," Ross remarked.

Ashe nodded to the outer world. "I suggest we make a strategic withdrawal. These may be nocturnal, too, but I'd rather not tangle with another in the jungle."

13

"DID YOU think we'd find *no* nasty surprises?" Ross drummed on the mess table with his scarred hand, his eyes showing amusement, even if his lips did not curve into a smile. "Let me share with you a small drop of good common sense, fella. It's just when things look the smoothest that there's a big trap waiting ahead on the trail."

Travis rubbed his bruised thigh. The other's humor grated. And since he had had time to consider the late battle, he began to suspect that he *had* been a little too sure of himself when he had entered the red-walled building. That didn't make him any more receptive to Ross's implied criticism, though—or what he chose to believe was criticism.

"You know"—Renfry came in from the corridor talking to Ashe—"those blue flying things came back twice while you were gone. They flew almost up to the port, but not inside.''

Travis, recalling the claws with which those were equipped, grunted. "Might be just as well," he commented.

"Then," Renfry said, paying no attention to his interruption, "just before you came back I found this—inside the outer lock.''

"This" was clearly no natural curiosity such as might have been deposited on their doorstep by some freak of the wind. Three green leaves possessing yellow ribs and veins had been pinned together with two-inch thorns into a cornucopia holder, a holder filled with oval, pale-green objects about the size of a thumbnail.

They could be fruit, seeds, a form of grain. Oddly enough, Travis was sure they were food of a sort. And plainly, too, they were an offering—a gesture of friendship—an overture on the part of the blue flyers. Why? For what purpose?

"You didn't see a flyer leave it?" questioned Ashe.

"No. I went to the port—and there it was.''

One of the seed things had dropped out of the packet, rolled across the table. Travis put a fingertip to it and the globe promptly burst as does an over-ripe grape when pressed. Without thinking, he raised his sticky finger to his mouth. The taste was tart, yet sweet, with the fresh cleanness of mint or some like herb.

"Now you've done it," observed Ross. "Well, we can watch while you break out in purple spots, or turn all green and shrivel up." His words were delivered in his usual amused tone, but there was a heat beneath that Travis did not understand. Unless once more Ross believed the Apache had taken too much on himself in that unthinking experiment.

"Good flavor," he returned with stolid defiance. And deliberately he chose another, transferring it to his mouth and breaking the skin with his teeth. The berry, or seed, or whatever it was, did not satisfy his desire for fresh meat, but it was not a concentrate or something out of one of the aliens' cans and the taste was good.

"That is enough!" Ashe swept up the leaf bag and its contents. "We'll have no more unnecessary chances taken."

But when Travis experienced no ill effects from his sampling, they shared out the rest of the gift at the evening meal, relishing the flavor after their weeks of the ship's supplies.

"Maybe we can trade for some more of these," Ross had begun almost idly. Then he gave a start and sat straighter in the uncomfortable mess seat.

Ashe laughed. "I wondered just when that possibility was going to dawn on you."

Ross grinned. "You may well ask. You'd think nothing stuck long between my ears, wouldn't you? All right—so we set up as traders again. I never did get a good chance to try out my techniques when we were on the Beaker run—too many interruptions."

Travis waited patiently for them to explain. This was another of those times when their shared experiences from the past shut him out, to remind him that only chance had brought him into this adventure, after all.

"There ought to be some things among all that stuff we routed out to study which should attract attention." Ross wriggled around Ashe to leave the mess cabin. "I'll see."

"Trade, eh?" Renfry nodded. "Heard how you boys on the time runs play that angle."

"It's a good cover, one of the best there is. A trader moves around without question in a primitive world. Any little strangeness in his speech, his customs, his dress, can be legitimately accounted for by his profession. He is supposed to come from a distance, his contacts don't expect him to be like their fellow tribesmen. And a trader picks up news quickly. Yes, trade was a cover the project used from the first."

"You were a trader, back in time?" Travis asked.

Ashe appeared willing enough to talk of his previous ventures. "D'you ever hear of the Beaker Folk? There *were* traders for you—had their stations from Greece to Scotland during the early Bronze Age. That was my cover, in early Britain, and again in the Baltic. You can really be fascinated by such a business. My first partner might have retired a millionaire—or that period's equivalent to one." Ashe paused, his face closing up again, but Travis asked another question.

"Why didn't he?"

"The Reds located our station in that era. Blew it up. And themselves into the bargain because they gave us our fix on their own post when they did that." He might have been discussing some dry fact in a report—until you saw his eyes.

Travis knew that Ross was dangerous. He thought

now that Ashe probably could surpass his young subordinate in ruthless action, was there any need to do so. Ross came back, his hands full. He set out his selections for their appraisal.

There was a length of material—perhaps intended for a scarf—which they had found in one of the crew lockers. A small thread of a vivid purple barred the green length, both colors bright enough to rivet attention. Then there were four pieces of carved wood, a coral-shaded wood with flecks of gold. They were stylized representations of fern fronds or feathers, as far as the Terrans could tell, and Ashe believed they might be men in some game, though playing board and other pieces had not been located. Lastly was the plaque which could so mysteriously reproduce a picture of him for the one holding it. That Ashe pushed aside with a shake of head.

"That's too important. We needn't be too generous the first time, anyway. After all, we've only a small offering to top. Try the scarf and two of these."

"Put them in the port?" Ross asked.

"I'd say no. No use encouraging visitors. Use your judgment in picking out some place below."

Ashe might have told Ross to take the initiative in that venture, but he followed him out. Travis, his leg having given him a sudden severe twinge, retired to his bunk, to try out the healing properties that resting pad had to offer in the circumstances. He stripped off his suit, stretched out with a grimace or two, and relaxed.

He must have gone to sleep under the narcotic influence of the healing jelly which seeped out and over him, triggered by his need. When he roused, it was to find Ross pulling at him.

"What's the matter?"

Ross allowed him no time for protest. "Ashe's gone!" His face might be schooled and impassive, but little cold devils looked out of his eyes.

"Gone?" The drowsiness induced by the healing of the bunk did not make quick thinking easy. "Gone where?"

"That's what we have to find out. Get moving!"

Travis, his bruises and aches gone, dressed, buckled the arms belt Ross pushed into his hands. "Let's have the story."

Ross was already in the corridor, every line of his taut body expressing his impatience.

"We were out there—fixed up a trading stone. There were a couple of flyers watching us and we waited to see if they would come down. When they didn't, Ashe said we had better take cover, as if we were going on to the buildings. Ashe detoured around a fallen tree—I saw him go. I tell you—I saw him! Then he wasn't there—or anywhere!" Ross was clearly shaken well out of his cultivated imperviousness.

"A ground trap?" Travis gave the first answer probable as he followed Ross to the air lock. Renfry was there making fast two lengths of silky cord barely coarser than knitting yarn but which, as they had discovered earlier, possessed a surprising strength. So hitched to the ship, they could prowl the vicinity and yet leave a guide to their whereabouts.

"I crawled over that ground inch by inch," Ross said between set teeth. "Not so much as a worm or ant hole showing. He was there one minute—the next he wasn't!''

Making fast their lines and leaving Renfry as lookout, they descended into the trampled and blasted area about the globe where the green was now withering under a sun not far from setting. Darkness would complicate their search. They had better move swiftly, find some clue before they were so baffled.

Ross took the lead, balancing along a fallen tree trunk to its crown of dropping fern fronds, now crushed and broken. "He was right here."

Travis swung down into the crushed foliage. The sharp smell of sticky sap, as well as the heavy scents of flowers and leaves, was cloying. But Ross was right. The vegetation on the ground had been pulled away in a wide sweep, and there was no sign that the dank earth beneath had been disturbed. He sighted a round-toes track, but it was twin to the ones he was leaving in the mold and could have been pressed there by either Ashe or Ross. But, because it was the only possible trace, he turned in the direction it pointed.

A moment or two later, at the very edge of the clearing Ross had made during his search, Travis saw something else. There was another tree trunk lying there, the remains of a true forest giant. And it had not been brought down by the landing of the ship, but had lain there long enough for soil and fallen leaves to build up about it, to grow a skin or red-capped moss or fungi.

Across that moss there were now two dark marks, ragged scars, suggesting that someone or something had clawed for a desperate hold against irresistible force. Ashe? But how had he been captured without Ross's seeing or hearing his struggles?

Travis vaulted the tree trunk. There was his confirmation—another footprint deep in the mold. But beyond it—nothing—absolutely nothing! And no living creature could have continued along that stretch of soft earth without leaving a trace. From this point it did appear that Ashe had vanished into thin air.

Air! Not on the ground but above it was where they would have to search. Travis called to Ross. There were tall trees about them now, trees with twenty feet or more of smooth bole before their first fern branches broke from the trunks. The wind rustled there, but they could sight no movement that was not normal, hear no sounds aloft.

Then one of the blue flyers came along, hovering over Travis, watching him with all four of its stalked eyes. The flyers—had they taken Ashe? He couldn't believe that. A man of Ashe's weight and strength, undoubtedly struggling hard into the bargain—at least the scrapping on the moss suggested that—could not have been airborne unless by a large flock of the blue creatures working together. But the Apache believed as completely as if he had witnessed it, that Ashe had been taken away either through the air or along a road of treetops.

"How did they get him up?" Ross puzzled. He appeared willing to accept Travis' idea, but the Apache, in turn, was forced to agree such a maneuver would be difficult. "And getting up," the time agent continued, "where in the world did they take him?"

"This lies in the opposite direction from the three nearest buildings." Travis pointed out. "To transport a prisoner might force them to travel in a direct line to their own quarters—speed would matter more than concealment."

"Which means a direct strike out into the jungle." Ross eyed the wilderness of trees, vines and brush with disfavor. "Well, there's one little trick—let me have your belt. This was something they showed us in basic training—good old basic." He took Travis' belt, made it fast to his own, increasing its expansion to the last hole before he measured it about the tree. But the girth of the bole was too great. Ross untied his cord connecting with the ship, slashed off a length to incorporate in the circle of belts. This time it served, uniting him to the bole. With the belt to support him, he hitched up the trunk which overhung the signs of struggle.

The fronds shook as he forced his way between them. "Here's your clue," he called down. "There's been a rope strung about this limb—worn a groove in the bark. And—Well, well, well—they're not so bright, after all—or they don't think we are. Here's a way to travel, all right—and by the upper reaches. Come up and see!"

A line made of cord and belts slapped down the trunk and Travis caught at it, making the climb with less agility than Ross had shown, to join the other at his perch among the fronds. He found the agent folding up between his hands another rope, but a supple green one which aped the vines native to this aeriel place.

"You do a Tarzan act." Ross flipped the rope end for emphasis. "Swing over to that tree, probably find another rope end there—and so on. I still don't see how they boosted Ashe along. Though"—his eyes narrowed—"maybe they waited to go until I went back to the ship for you."

Travis eyed the rope. "Leaving that here means one thing—"

"That they intend to return?" Ross nodded. "They may have some bright plans about scooping us up one by one. But who are 'they'? Not those blue flyers. . . ."

"Those might act as their hounds." Travis tried not to glance at the ground, for his present perch inspired little confidence in him.

"And that fruit present was bait for a trap," Ross agreed. "It fits. The fruit to get us out of the ship, the flyers to report when we came. Then—pounce!— one of us is snaffled! Only Ashe isn't going to stay a prisoner."

"This could be a trap, too," Travis reminded him as he gave the rope a jerk and discovered Ross had been right, the line was very firmly attached to its tree anchorage.

"True enough. But we'll find some way."

"At night?" The sun was close to setting. Travis wanted to be on the trail just as much as Ross, but common sense would pay off better than a reckless dash to the rescue.

"Night—" Ross squinted at the patches of sunlight. "These things move around in the daytime. And they're used to heights."

"Which suggests there may be good reasons for not traveling on the ground or in the dark." Travis was growing a little tired of talking. "Our friend in the red house may be one of those reasons. What is your solution?"

"We go back to the domed place—up to the top. There is a balcony around the dome itself, and we can take our bearings from there."

Travis could agree with that. But they had to argue down the protests of Renfry. The technician's demands to accompany them Ross was able to overcome by pointing out crisply that alone of their party Renfry possessed the knowledge, or fraction of knowledge, which might mean their eventual control of the ship, and so of their future. And the need for a scouting party before dark urged the necessity for speed in their try to locate landmarks which might guide them on a hunt for Ashe.

They threaded the path they had cut that morning. Travis glanced now and then at the sky when they crossed small glades. He had half expected to find the blue flyers on the lookout. But none appeared.

Ross took the inner ramp under the dome at a rapid trot. His pace, however, slowed as they wound their way up past five levels, then six, seven, eight, nine and finally ten. There was no sound in the building, nothing to break the echoing emptiness of the fantastically beautiful shell.

They reached the balcony, a narrow walk curving completely around the bulk of the dome, protected by a breast-high parapet of the carved lace. The wind, now rising in intensity, pulled at their hair, sang weirdly through the openwork. Ross took the lead. He hurried to the vantage point from which they could obtain an unrestricted view in the direction they thought Ashe's captors had headed.

There were other buildings, or the remains of buildings, rising out of the jungle. Some of them were smaller than the dome, three or four—at a greater distance—taller. And the taller ones had a certain similarity of outline which suggested that they must have had a common architectural origin.

It was one of those which Ross indicated now. "If they were headed for the nearest building across the treetops—that must be it." He sighted along his pointed finger as he might have along a rifle barrel.

Travis was listing all possible landmarks—though from ground level perhaps three-quarters of them would not be of much use. "To the right of that funnel-shaped capping, and the left of the pile of blocks. It may be several miles from here."

To cut a trail along the ground was possible—using their blasters. But such action would certainly advertise their coming. If they wanted to locate the enemy—always providing, of course, that the enemy *was* roosting in the structure Ross had just chosen—the process must entail a longer and more complicated bit of trail craft. And such a scout could not be made at night.

"There's one way of checking," Ross said, as if he were thinking aloud. "If we stay here until dark, we'd know."

"How?"

"Lights. If we see any lights out there—they would be proof."

"Slim chance. They'd be fools to use lights."

"Could be trap-setting again," Ross demurred. "More bait to pull us in."

"That's just guessing. How can we tell what makes their minds tick? We don't even know what they are. You didn't like the type who first wore this uniform." Travis plucked at the blue fabric crossing his chest. "If this was their home planet, wouldn't they be able to play games with us the way they did with you—by mental control?"

"Look out there!" Ross's sweep of hand included half the landscape, the sea of untroubled jungle, the buildings rising in isolated islands out of it. "Whatever they had—it's dead now—long dead. And maybe they're dead, too—or back at the primitive stage. If they're primitives, Ashe can handle them to a point; he's been taught to do just that. I've seen him in action. Give me an hour up here past sundown. Then if we see no lights—I'll go. . . ."

Travis drew his blaster. Dark, or even heavy dusk, here might unleash things to lurk in the shadows along their trail. But he could understand Ross's point, and they had a well-marked path to the ship.

"All right."

They walked slowly around the dome waiting for the murk of evening to gather. And so they counted at least fifty more buildings, fantastic, unlike, some even appearing to defy the laws of gravity. Beyond them were those others, tall, thin, of a common mold. Were those the native structures and these others embassies, examples of trans-galactic architecture as Ashe had suggested? If not all of them were stripped, what a wealth of knowledge lay—

Travis was jerked out of speculation by a cry from Ross. There was still a reflection of sunlight in the sky at their backs. But—Murdock's hunch had paid off. A wink of light flashed across the green from the first of the distant tall towers. Flashed on—off—on.

Was it meant to be an enticing signal?

14

THEY HELD a council of war in the ship, the outer
hatch closed against the night, that simple precaution
taught them by the desert world.

"It'll be difficult to go straight through the tangle
in that direction," Renfry observed. "They'd be
waiting for you to try it."

"Sometimes the fastest way is around, not
straight," Ross agreed. He had a map drawn on a
sheet of material from the aliens' stores, the crosses
and squares on it marking the various buildings they
had sighted. "See here—they bunch, those tall towers. But here, and here, and here, are other buildings. Suppose we head for this one which looks like
an outsized oil can, then beyond that there's the pile
of blocks. The one we want is between them. So—
move to the funnel top, then start beyond to the block
pile—and cut back. If we can make them believe

we're just searching everything in that direction, it'll buy us time. Reach a point about here"—his forefinger dug into the surface of the improvised map—"and then do a right-about-face and go at top speed." He looked up challengingly. "Anybody got a better idea?"

Renfry shrugged. "This is your party, you've had the training for this type of thing. But I'll go along."

"And let some joker take the ship behind our backs?" Ross wanted to know. "They've a line on us—they must have or they wouldn't have scooped up the chief so neatly. He's no recruit at this type of fun and games, remember. I've seen him in action."

"Through the treetops," Travis mused. "If that's their regular mode of travel, then maybe we have another point in our favor. Once we're really into the jungle, there's a lot of cover which will give us protection. They can't watch us from above all the time."

"You're both set on this then?" Renfry still studied the map.

Ross stood up. "I don't propose to let them nobble the chief and get away with it. And the quicker we are on the move—the better!"

But even Ross had to admit that they must wait until dawn to put their plan to the test. They rummaged the ship for supplies and assembled a small pack apiece. Each wore a belt supporting alien blasters. In addition a coil of the supple cord-rope was wound from shoulder to hip about their bodies, and they had retained the flint knives from their hunter disguise. Brittle though the flint might be, the finely chipped blades could still serve a deadly purpose in close combat. They slung packsacks with food and the froth containers.

Renfry disputed his staying with the ship. But he was forced to admit that there was no way to lock the port behind them and so a guard must remain. However, he insisted upon triggering the armament of the spacer. So when they descended the ladder to the ground in the first dull rose of the early morning, the black mouths of those sinister tubes were thrust from the shell of the globe.

They took turns cutting a path. And, where they could they pushed through the underbrush, saving the power of the blasters. It was Travis who led when they thrust completely through a fern wall into a green tunnel.

The ground here had been worn into a shallow trough and beaten hard. Travis needed only one look to know that slot for what it was—a game trial, leading either to water or to some favorite grazing ground. It had been well traveled, and for some length of time.

There were tracks here, pads with the pinprick indentations of claws well beyond them, a cloven hoof with so deep a cleavage that the hoof must be almost split in two, and some smaller tracings too alien to be identified.

"This goes in the right direction. Do we follow it?" Travis was in two minds about such an action himself. On one hand they could greatly increase their speed and speed might be important. But a well-used game trail not only provided a road for animals—it was as well a lure for those creatures that preyed upon such travelers.

Ross moved out on the narrow path. It had twists and turns, but the way did run in the direction of the funnel top which was their first goal.

"We do," he decided.

Travis dropped into a loose trot which fitted his feet into the slot of the track. He caught small sounds in the vegetation about them—twitters, squeaks, sometimes a harsh, croaking call. But he saw nothing of the creatures that voiced them.

The trail took a dip into a shallow ravine. At the bottom a stream trickled lazily over brown-green gravel and above them the sky was open. There they disturbed a fisher.

Travis' hand went to the grip of his blaster, dropped away again. Like the blue flyers, this strange inhabitant of the unknown world gave no impression of hostility. The beast was about the size of a wild cat, and somewhat similar to a cat in appearance. At least, it possessed a round head with eyes set slightly aslant. But the ears very very long and sharply pointed with heavy tufts of—feathers at their tips. Feathers! The blue flyer had been furred, provided with insect wings. The fisher, plainly a ground dweller, was fluffily clothed in soft feathers of the same blue-green shade as the foliage about. Had it not been crouched on the rock in the open, it would have passed unseen.

Its haunches and hind legs were heavy and it squatted back upon them. Two pairs of far more slender and longer front limbs held a limp, scaled thing which it had been methodically denuding of a series of fringe legs by the aid of teeth and claws. Interrupted, the animal watched Travis with round-eyed interest, displaying neither alarm nor anger at his sudden appearance.

As the Terran edged forward, the creature freed one front leg, still clasping its prey in the other three, and flicked a fringe leg or two from its feather-clad paunch in absent-minded tidiness. Then folding its breakfast to its middle with the intermediary pair of arms or forepaws, it leaped spectacularly from a sitting position, to be hidden in the brush.

"Rabbit—cat—owl—whatsis," Ross commented. "Wasn't afraid though."

"Means that it either hasn't any enemies—or none resembling us." Travis studied the curtain into which the fisher had plunged. "Yes, it's still watching—from over there," he added in a half whisper.

But the presence of the feather-clad feaster was in a way a promise of security along this road. Travis found the opening of the trail on the other side of the stream. And he was now better pleased to follow it, even though once more the tree ferns closed in overhead and he and Ross were swallowed in what was a tight tunnel of green.

The indications of a busy, hidden life about them continued to come in sounds. Twice they stumbled on evidence of some hunter or hunters working the trail. Once they found a fluff of plush-like gray fur still bedaubed with light pinkish blood, then a clot of cream-yellow feathers and draggled skin.

There was an open apron about the funnel building. A fan of stone, dappled with red moss but not yet claimed in entirety by the jungle and the game trail, skirted this, running on past the building. If they were to continue to follow Ross' plan, they must strike back now into the jungle again and bull their way through its resilient mass. But first, for the benefit of any watchers, they crossed that moss-spattered apron to the building as if about to search its interior. Only there was no easy entrance here. A grill, of the same imperishable material as that which formed the fan area before the door, forbade their entry. Through its bars they could see parts of the inside. Plainly this particular structure had been left furnished after a fashion, for objects, muffled in disintegrating coverings, crowded the floor.

Ross, his face pressed close to the bars, whistled. "I'd say they were getting ready for movers, only the vans never arrived. The chief'll want to break in here, might be some of his kind of pickings about."

"Better collect *him* first." Travis stood at the top of those four wide steps leading to the barred door. He could sight the tower which was their ultimate goal, though the fern trees shielded it for about three stories up. To his survey there were no signs of life about it, nothing moved at any of the window holes. Yet there had been that light at yesterday's dusk.

"All right—we'll get to it!" Ross came away from the grill. He swung his arm wide in an extravagant gesture to mark not the goal of their choice but the block building beyond it.

They had to cut their way now, using blasters and their hands to pull and break a path between the small, isolated glades where the fall of some giant tree in the past had cleared a passable strip for them.

Panting and floundering, they came to the fifth such clearing.

"This is it," Ross said. "We'll turn back from here."

Luckily the summit of the tower showed now and then as a guide. They were approaching it from the back, and by some freakish whim of nature there was less underbrush here. So they had to choose cover, watching the heights for any indication that some scout or spy might lurk aloft. Not that they could be certain of spotting any army under the circumstances, Travis decided gloomily, moving with the wariness of one expecting an ambush at any moment.

They had covered perhaps half of the distance which would bring them to the base of the tower when both of them were startled into immobility by a squall. The battle cry of the thing which had laired in the red hall! And the sound was so distorted by the jungle about them that Travis could not tell whether its source lay before or behind.

That first wail of battle was only the starting signal of a racket, a din to split Terran eardrums. A bird thing boomed out of the brush, flew in blind panic straight for the two, blundered past them in safety. A graceful, slender creature with a dappled coat and a single curving horn flashed away before Travis was truly sure he had seen it.

But those howls of rage and blood hunger chorused on. There must be more than one of the beasts—perhaps a pack of them! And from the noise, they were engaged in combat. Travis could only think of Ashe cornered in the tower to face such an enemy. He began to run. Ross drew level with him before they plunged together into a hedge of brush, fighting their way in the straightest line to the base of the tower.

Travis tripped, staggered forward, fighting to regain his balance, and plowed on his hands and knees into the open. He was facing the entrance to the tower, a long, narrow slit of opening. From within came the sounds. Ross, blaster in hand, leaped past him, a blue streak of concentrated action.

The Apache scrambled up, was only a step or two behind the time agent as they entered, finding themselves directly on the foot of an upward-leading ramp. One of those squalling roars, sounding above, ended in a cough. A mass of dull red fur, flailing legs, a flat, narrow, weasel's head showing snapping jaws, rolled down, struggling in convulsive death agony. Ross leaped aside.

"Blaster got that one!" he shouted. "Chief! Ashe! You up there?"

If there was any answer to that hail, the words were drowned in the screech of the animals. The light was dusky here, but there was enough for the Terrans to spot the barrier across the ramp. It was a barrier which had been there some time but was now showing a gap, choked by two of the red beasts struggling against each other in their eagerness to force that doorway. Behind them snarled a third.

Travis steadied the barrel of the blaster across his forearm and nicked a darting weasel-head with a sniper's expert aim. The thing did not even cry out, but reared, somersaulted backward down the ramp as the men jumped apart to give it room.

One of the creatures at the gap caught sight of the two below and pulled back, allowing its fellow through the barrier while it whirled to spring at Ross. His blaster beam raked across its shoulders and it screamed hideously, collapsed, scratching frantically with its hind feet to gain footing. Ross fired again and the animal was still. But the rage of the fight beyond the barrier continued.

"Ashe!" Ross shouted. And Travis, catching his breath, echoed that call. To go through the gap in the barrier before them and perhaps be met by a blaster beam from a friend was certainly not to be desired.

"Hullloooo!" The cry was weirdly echoed, dehumanized, and it appeared to come from some distance ahead or above. But both of them had heard it and now they pushed past the barrier into a wide hallway.

There was light here, coming in white flames from smoking brands which lay on the floor at the far end as if tossed from a higher level. One of the red beasts lay dead and they hurdled the body. Another, dragging useless hindquarters, crept with deadly purpose toward them and Travis picked it off. But the beam in his blaster died before he lifted a finger from firing button. Another try proved his fears correct—the charge in the weapon was exhausted.

There was a scrambling on the second ramp at the far end of the hall. Ross stood at the foot, his blaster up. Travis stooped to scoop up one of the torches. He whirled the brand in the air, bringing the smoldering end into a burst of life.

Ross aimed at a charging weasel-head, missed, flung himself to the side of the ramp and over to the floor to escape the rush. But the beast plunged insanely after him. Travis whirled the torch a second time, bringing its flaming end down in a swing against the snaky, darting head of the attacker.

One of those powerful forepaws aimed a vicious swipe, tore the torch from the Apache's hold. But Ross was up to his knees again, blaster ready. And the red animal died. Travis retreated, a little unsteadily, to pick up a second torch.

"Hullloooo!" Again that shout from overhead. Ross answered it.

"Ashe! Down here. . . ."

There were no more squalls from the ramp. But Travis wondered if more of the beasts lay in wait. With a useless blaster he had no desire to climb into the unknown. A flint knife was nothing against the weasel-heads.

They waited, listening, at the foot of the ramp. But when there came no other attack, Ross pattered ahead and Travis followed, nursing his new torch. His hand shot out, closed on Ross's arm, as he caught up with the other. Something was waiting for them up there.

Travis thrust the torch into that pocket of gloom at the head of the ramp, saw Ross's blaster at ready—

"Come on in!" The words were ordinary enough, but Ashe's voice sounded a little breathless and in higher pitch than usual. But it *was* Ashe, unharmed and seeming his usual self, who stepped into the pool of light and waited for them to join him. Only he was not alone. Half-seen shadows moved behind him. Ross did not holster his blaster and Travis' hand rested on his knife helt.

"You all right, chief?"

Ashe laughed in answer to Ross's demand. "Now that the space patrol has landed, yes. You boys introduced the right play at the proper moment. Come on and meet the gang."

The torch sputtered as those shadows moved in closer to Ashe. Then a new light blazed up well above floor level and Travis blinked at the company that fire revealed.

Ashe was six feet tall, giving Travis himself an inch or so. But in this company he towered, for the tallest of his companions came only a little above his shoulder.

"They have wings!"

Yes, with a sudden twitch a flap of wing—not feathered, but ribbed skin—had unfurled, pointing up above its owner's shoulder. Where had he seen a wing such as that? On the statue from the domed building!

However, the faces now all turned toward the Terrans were not as grotesque as the one of the image. The ears were not so large, the features were more humanoid, though the noses remained vertical slits. Either the statue had been a caricature, or it represented a far more primitive type.

The natives hung back, and from their narrow, pointed jaws came a low murmur, rising and falling, which Travis could not separate into distinct sounds or words.

"Local inhabitants?" Ross still held his blaster. "They the ones who kidnapped you, chief?"

"In a manner of speaking. I take it you accounted for the wild life below?"

"All we saw," Travis returned, still watching the winged people, for they were people, of that he was sure.

"Then we can get out of here." Ashe turned to the waiting shadows and holstered his own weapon with an emphatic slam. Two of the winged men beckoned and the rest stood back, allowing Ashe, Ross and Travis to pass them, to climb a third ramp. At the top the Terrans saw the open yellow of sunlight, and came out into a wide hall with archways, not doors, down its length.

Travis' nostrils expanded as he caught a mixture of scents, some pleasant, some otherwise. There was activity here; there were indications that this was a permanent settlement. The archways were hung with nets of green into which were tucked flowers here and there, many like the one he had found on his first day of exploration. Logs, hollowed out and so made into troughs, stood about the walls. From them grew a mixture of plants, all reaching toward the sun which came through windows, running a curtain of green from floor level to ceiling.

The people were no longer just shadows. And in this brighter light their humanoid resemblance was marked. The furled wings covered their backs as might folded cloaks, and they wore no clothing save ornaments of belt, collar or armlets. The weapons, which all within sight carried, were small spears— little enough protection against the red killers which had assailed them from below.

They watched the Terrans closely, keeping up their murmur of speech, but making no threatening gestures. And since it was impossible for the Terrans to read any expression on their faces, Travis did not know whether the three from the ship were considered prisoners, allies, or merely strange objects of general interest.

"Here. . . ." Ashe stopped before one of the curtained archways and pursed his lips to give a gentle hoot.

The curtain parted and he went in, signaling the other two to follow him.

Under their feet was thick matting plaited from vines and leaves. And there were low partitions of lattice work over which living plants climbed to form dividing walls, cutting one large room into a series of smaller cubicles around a central space fronting the archway.

"Pay attention to nothing around the wall," Ashe said quickly. "Keep your eyes on the one at the table."

Squatting by a table raised some two feet from the carpeted floor was one of the winged men. Those they had seen in the outer hallway had had skins which were a dusky lavender color, close in shade to the very stone from which the image had been carved. But this one was darker, almost a deep purple. And there was something in his constrained movements which suggested the stiffness of age.

But when the native looked up to meet Ashe's gaze in welcome, Travis knew that this was not only a man, but a great man among his kind. It was there in his eyes, in the pride of his carriage, and in the slow deliberation of the searching study with which he regarded the three Terrans.

15

"WHAT A junkyard!" Ross stared about him in sheer stupefaction.

"Treasure house!" his chief corrected him almost sharply.

Travis simply stood between them and gazed. Perhaps both descriptions could apply in part.

"They kidnapped you to sort *this* out for them?" Ross demanded, as if he couldn't believe a word of that conclusion.

"That's the general idea," Ashe admitted. "Question is—where do we start, what do we have, and how can we get across to them the meaning of anything we do find—if we can make it out ourselves?"

"How long have they been collecting all this?" Travis wondered. There were paths through those piles of moldering materials, so one *could* investigate the contents of the heaps. But the general confusion of the mass was almost intimidating.

Ashe shrugged. "When your total method of communication consists of gestures, a lot of ragged guessing, and pointing, how is anyone to know anything?"

"But why you? I mean—how are you supposed to know what makes all this tick, or thump, or otherwise run?" Ross asked again.

"We came in the ship. They may have some hazy tradition—legends—that the ship people knew everything."

"The Fair Gods," Travis threw in.

"Only we are not Cortez and his men," Ashe returned with a snap.

"They aren't the baldies, or that furry-faced operator I saw on the vision plate of the ship the Reds had. So where do they fit in?"

"Judging by the statue, their ancestors were known to the builders of the dome," Ashe replied. "But I think they are primitive, not decadent."

Travis' imagination made a sudden, swift leap.

"Pets?"

Both of the others looked at him. Ashe drew a deep breath.

"You might just be right!" The way he spaced his words gave them an impressive emphasis. "Give our world ten thousand years and the right combination of conditions and see what could happen to our dogs or our cats."

"Are we prisoners?" Ross came back to a main point.

"Not now. Our handling of the weasels took care of that. A common enemy is an excellent argument for mutual peace. And we have a common purpose here, too. If we're going to find out anything which will help Renfry, it will be in just such a collection as this."

"It'd take a year just to shuffle through the top layer in this mess," Ross gave a gloomy opinion.

"We know what we are looking for—we have examples on the ship. Anything we can uncover in the process which might help our winged friends, we turn over to them. And who knows what we may find?"

Ashe was right about the attitude of the winged people. The chief or leader, who had first received them in the vine-walled room and brought them in turn into the huge chamber containing the loot gathered by his tribe, showed no unwillingness to let them return to the ship. But their path back, followed on ground and not by the aeriel ways of the natives, was supervised by two of the blue flyers that had some link with the winged people—perhaps a relationship not unlike man and hound.

During his period of captivity Ashe had learned that the red weasels were the principal local menace and that the winged fold had tried to wall off the lower sections of their dwelling towers to baffle the hunters. These creatures had worked with sly cunning—which suggested a measure of intelligence on their part also—on the ramp barrier. But only a determined raid made by a whole pack had finally broken through that laboriously constructed wall to get at the living quarters of the flying people. Ashe's readiness to use his blaster on the behalf of his captors and the surprise attack by Ross and Travis had completely destroyed the marauding pack. These two things had also made a favorable impression upon the intended victims. As Ashe had commented, a common enemy was a firm base on which to build an alliance.

"But they can fly," Ross protested. "Why didn't they just take off—out the windows, and let those six-legged weasels have the place?"

"For a reason their chief was finally able to make plain. This is apparently the season during which their young are born. The males could have escaped, but the females and young could not."

They found Renfry awaiting their arrival at the ship in fingernail-gnawing state of impatience. Relieved to see them whole and together, he greeted them with the news that he had managed to trace the routing of the trip tape through the control board. Whether he could reset another tape, or reverse the present one, he did not yet know.

"I don't know about rewinding this one." He tapped the coin-sized disk they had seen ejected from the board on the morning of their arrival. "If the wire breaks—" He shrugged and did not need to elaborate.

"So you'd like to have another to practice on." Ashe nodded. "All right, we all know what to look for when we start our digging into the treasure trove tomorrow."

"If any still exist." Renfry sounded dubious.

"Deduction number one." Ashe took a long pull from the froth-drink can. "I believe most of the stuff the winged folk have gathered came from towers such as the one they use to house their village. And there are a number of those here. The other buildings of radically different design are not duplicated. Which leads you to surmise that the tower structures are native to this planet, the other types imported for some purpose.

"When that pilot set the control tape to bring the ship here, he was setting course either for his home—or his service headquarters. Therefore, it is not too improbable to suppose that we can hope to come across something in that miscellaneous mixture of loot they've gathered which is allied to record tapes we have found on this ship. And I will not rule out journey wires among the litter."

"There are a lot of ifs, ands, and maybes in that," Renfry said.

Ashe laughed. "Man, I have been dealing with ifs and maybes for most of my adult life. Being a snooper into the past takes a lot of guessing—then the hard grind of working to prove your guesses are right. There are certain basic patterns which become familiar—which you can use as the framework for your guess."

"Human patterns," Travis reminded. "Here we do not deal with humans."

"No, we don't. Unless you widen the definition of human to include an entity with intelligence and the power to use it. Which I believe we shall have to do, now that we are no longer planet—or system—bound. Anyway, to hunt through the remains of the tower civilization is the first concrete job we have now."

The next morning found them all, Renfry included, back at the tower. And, in those patches of sunlight which entered the packed room, the job Ashe and the chief of the winged people had set them looked even more formidable.

That is—it did until the cubs, or chicks, or children of the natives turned up to offer busy hands and quick bright eyes to assist. Travis found himself the center of a small gathering of winged midgets, all watching him with eager attention as he tried to disentangle a pile of disintegrating objects. A pair of small hands swooped to catch a rolling container, another helper brought out a box. A third straightened a coil of flexible stuff which was snarled about the top layer of the pile. The Apache laughed and nodded, hoping that both gestures would be translated as thanks and encouragement. Apparently they were, for the youngsters dived in with a will, their small hands wriggling into places he could not reach. Twice, though, he had hurriedly to jerk some too-ambitious delver back from a threatened avalanche of heavy goods.

So much of what they uncovered, examined, and put to one side was either too badly damaged by time to be of any use, or else had no meaning for the Terrans. Travis struggled with the covers of crumbling containers and boxes. Sometimes he would see them go to dust with their contents under his prying hands; other times he would find their interiors filled only with powder which might once have been fabric.

Lengths of an alloy, fashioned into sections of pipe, he laid to one side. These seemed still intact and might be of use to the winged people, either as material for weapons more effective than their spears, or for tools. Once he came upon an oval box which flaked to bits in his hands, but it left mingled with the powder on his palm a glittering stone set in a scroll of metal, as untarnished and perfect as the day the jewel had been stored. His volunteer assistants hummed with wonder and he gave it to the nearest, to see it passed from hand to hand and at last gravely returned to his keeping.

By noon none of the four Terrans, working in opposite corners of the big room, had found anything useful to their own purposes. They met under a window to share food supplies free of the dust of the rubbish heap.

"I knew it was a year's job," Ross complained. "And what have we found so far? Some metal which hasn't rusted completely away, a few jewels—"

"And this." Ashe held out a round spool. "If I'm not mistaken, this is a record tape. And it may be intact. Looks something like those we found aboard the ship."

"Here comes the big boss," Ross said, glancing up. "Are you going to ask him for that?"

The chief who had brought them to this storeroom entered the far doorway with his escort. He moved slowly about the perimeter of the room to inspect the piles where the explorers had made such a small beginning. When he reached the Terrans they stood up, towering over both chief and escort. Though they did not share language and their communication was by gesture, Ashe went to work to suggest a few uses for the morning's salvage. The gems were understandable enough. And the metal tubes were examined politely without much interest.

Ashe spoke to Renfry across the chief's shoulder. "Any chance of working these into spears?"

"Given time—and tools—maybe." But the technician did not sound too certain.

Last of all Ashe displayed the spool, and for the first time the chief became animated. He took it into his own hands and hummed to one of the guards who went off at a trot. He tapped one finger on the red tape and then spread out all the digits several times, ending with a wide inclusive sweep of one arm.

"What's he trying to tell us, Ashe?" Renfry had been watching the performance closely.

"I think he means that this is only one of many. We may have made a real discovery."

The guard came back followed by a smaller, younger edition of himself. Taller than the children, the newcomer was probably an adolescent. He saluted the chief with a clap of his wings and stood waiting until his leader held out the spool. Then, reaching out, the chief caught at Ashe's hand and put the youngster's in it—waving them off together.

"You going?" Ross wanted to know.

"I will. I think they want to show us where this came from. Renfry, you had better come too. You might be able to recognize a technical record better than I could."

When they were gone, the chief and his retinue after them, Ross looked about him with dissatisfaction written plain on his face.

"There's nothing worth grubbing for here."

Travis had picked up a length of the tubing, to

examine it in the full light of the window. The section was four feet or so long and showed no signs of erosion or time damage. An alloy, it was light and smooth, and what its original use had been he did not know. But as he ran it back and forth through his hands an idea was born.

The winged men needed better weapons than the spears. And to make such weapons from the odds and ends of metals they had found in this litter required forging methods perhaps none of the Terrans, not even Renfry, had the skill to teach. But there was one arm which could be made—and perhaps even the ammunition for it might also exist in the unclassified masses on the floor. It was not a weapon his own people had used, but to the south those of his race had developed it into a deadly and accurate arm.

"What's so special about that tube?" Ross asked.

"It might be special—for these people." Travis held it up, put one end experimentally to his lips. Yes, it was light enough to be used as he planned.

"In what way?"

"Didn't you ever hear of blowguns?"

"What?"

"The main part is a tube such as this—they're used mostly by South American Indians. A small splinter arrow is blown through and they are supposed to be accurate and deadly. Sometimes poisoned arrows are used. But the ordinary kind would do if you hit a vital point, say one of those weasel's eyes—or its throat."

"You begin to make sense, fella." Ross hunted

for a section of pipe to match Travis'. "You plan to give these purple people a better way to kill red weasels. Can you make one to really work?"

"We can always try." Travis turned to the clustering children and gestured, getting across the idea that such sections of pipe were now of importance. The junior assistants scattered with excited hums as if he had loosed a swarm of busy bees in the room.

As Travis had hoped, he was also able to discover the necessary material for arrows there. Again their original use was unknown, but at the end of a half hour's search he had a handful of needle-slim slivers of the same light alloy as the pipes themselves. Since he had never built or used a blowgun and knew the principles of the weapon only through reading, he looked forward to a period of trial and error. But at last they gleaned from the room a wealth of raw materials with which to experiment. And they had not yet done when the youngster who had guided Ashe came back, to tug at Ross's sleeve and beckon the Terrans to follow.

They wound from one ramp to another, passing the point where the weasels had breached. But they did not leave the tower. Instead their guide went to the back of the entrance hall, putting both hands to a seemingly blank wall and pushing. Travis and Ross, watching his effort, joined their strength to his and a panel slipped back into the wall.

Before them was not a room, but a more sharply inclined ramp descending into a well of shadow which increased in darkness until its foot could not be sighted from their present stand. The winged boy took the downward path at a run. His wings expanded until they balanced his body and he skimmed at a speed neither of the Terrans was reckless enough to try to match.

Once they reached the foot of the descent, they saw in the distance the smoky gleam of one of the native torches. And, guided by that, they ran along a narrow corridor where dust rose in puffs under their pounding feet.

The room of plunder in the tower above had housed unsorted heaps of bits and pieces. The place they now entered, where Ashe awaited them, was a monument to the precision and efficiency of the same race—or a kindred people—of those who flew the ship.

Here were machines, banks of controls, dim, dark vision plates. And as the Terrans advanced slowly the torch displayed racks and racks of containers, not only of record tapes, but of journey disks. Hundreds, thousands of those button spools which had brought them across space, were racked in cylinders with transparent tops and unknown symbols of the other people on their labels.

"Port control center—we think." Ashe may have temporized by adding those last two words, but there was a certainty in his tone which suggested he was sure. Renfry was filling the front of his suit with samples taken from both record containers and tape racks.

"Library. . . ." Travis added an identification of his own.

Ashe nodded. "If we only knew what to take! Lord, maybe everything we want, we need—not only for now but for the whole future—is right here!"

Ross went to the nearest rack, began to follow Renfry's example.

"We can try to run these on the reader in the ship. And if we take enough of them, the odds are at least one or two should be helpful."

His logical approach to the problem was the sensible one. They went about the selection as methodically as they could, lifting samples from each rack of holders.

"A whole galaxy of knowledge must be stored here," Ashe marveled, as his fingers flicked one coil after another free.

They left at last, the fronts of their flexible suits bulging, their hands full. But before they left the tower, Travis also gathered up the lengths of pipe and the needle slivers. And when they were back in the ship, the reader set up, their plundered record rolls ready to feed, the Apache went to work on fashioning the weapon he hoped to offer to the winged people in return for their sharing of the stored wisdom.

Renfry, an array of small tools from the crew lockers aligned before him, was operating on one of the route disks. He was prying off its cover and carefully unwinding the thin wire spiral curled within. Twice he was doomed to disappointment, that fragile thread upon which a ship could cruise to the stars snapping brittlely under his most careful handling. The second time that happened he looked up, his face drawn, his eyes red with strain.

"I don't think it can be done."

"There's this." Ashe reached for one of the waiting disk tapes. "Those you are working with are old. The one in the ship is new."

There it was again, the jog in time which might return them to their own world—or might not. But that reminder appeared to encourage Renfry. He checked the outside of his disks, pushing aside any which showed the pitting of years. His next choice did not look too different from the one which held their future locked into its spiral. For the third time he pried delicately to force off the case.

But it was not to be that night that they learned anything which was of value to them. The record tapes in the reader gave only a series of pictures, fascinating in themselves, but of no value now. And in addition there were others which merely flashed symbols—perhaps formulae, perhaps written. accounts. At last Ashe snapped off the machine.

"We can't expect to be lucky all the time."

"There're thousands of those things stored in that place," Ross pointed out. "If we do find anything useful—it will have to be by luck!"

"Well, luck is what we have to count on in our game." Ashe's voice was tired, drained. He moved slowly, rubbing his hands across his eyes. "When you give up a belief in luck, you're licked!"

16

TRAVIS SET the mouthpiece of a blowgun to his lips and puffed. A thin, shining sliver, tipped with a fleecy tuft, sped—to center on his improvised target of a red-veined leaf and pin it more securely to the trunk of a fern tree some ten feet away. He was absurdly pleased with the success of his trial shot. He moved back another four feet and prepared for a second test. All the while the low humming of his enthralled native audience buzzed bee-fashion across the clearing.

When he was able to place a second dart almost beside the first, his satisfaction was close to complete. With a crooked finger Travis beckoned to the winged youth who had helped to carry the newly manufactured weapons to the testing ground. He handed over the tube he had just used, picking up a second, slightly longer, from the selection on the ground.

The young warrior laid his spear on the leaf mold, hooking his clawed toes over its shaft while he fumbled with the blowgun. Raising the weapon to his mouth, he gave a vigorous puff. Not as centered as Travis' shot had been, the sliver hit the tree slightly above the leaf. Two other natives, their wings unfolding slightly as they ran, hurried to inspect the target, and Travis, smiling and nodding, brought his hands together in a sharp clap of approval.

They needed no more urging to try this new weapon. Tubes were snatched, passed from hand to hand, with some squabbling on the outer fringes of the gathering. Then each took his turn to try shooting, with varying degrees of success. They halted from time to time to pick the target clean of ammunition, or put up another leaf over the tattered remnants of the last.

Several of Travis' pupils had sharpshooters' eyes, and the Apache believed that with practice they could far surpass his own efforts. When the midday sun bit down on the range, he left the blowguns with the enthusiastic marksmen and went to hunt up his crew mates.

Renfry was still buried in his study of journey tapes and the ship's circuits. But when Travis climbed to the control cabin he found Ashe there also. The reader was set up on the floor, and both of them were squatting before it, alternately watching some recording and making attacks on the main panel of the pilot's unit. The case of that had been removed, exposing an intricate wiring pattern. And

from time to time Renfry traced one of those threads
up or down and either beamed or frowned at the
results of his investigation.

"What's going on?"

Ashe answered Travis. "We may have had our
break! This record is a manual of sorts. It provides
some wiring blueprints Renfry has been able to identify with that cat's cradle of cords up there."

"*Some* wiring." Renfry's enthusiasm did not
match Ashe's at that moment. "About one line in
ten! This is like trying to put together a Nike head
when all your working instructions are written in
Chinese code! Yeah—the red cord hits the plate
there—but does it say anything about these white
loop-deloops to the left?"

Ashe squinted at the loops in question and con-
sulted the record reader again. "Yes!" Renfry was
down on his knees in an instant to see for himself the
diagram on the picture screen.

"Anybody home?" Ross's voice floated up the
well of the interior ladder, and Travis could feel the
vibration of his footfalls on the rungs as he climbed.

His head and shoulders emerged from the stairwell. His face was streaked with dust which testified
to his occupation of the morning as the investigator
on duty in the crazy treasure house at the winged
people's tower.

"Any luck?" Travis asked with some sympathy.
Ross shrugged.

"A handful of stuff they may be able to use. I'm
no big brain to string together some wire, nails and a
couple of pieces of tin and produce an A-jet all set to
fly. Saw your William Tells busy with those spitters

of theirs. One of them had already bagged an addition to the dinner pot—not that the dear departed looked too edible. I don't care for things with about four dozen legs all clawing at once. But I could relish some more civilized food right now.''

Travis glanced at Ashe and the dedicated Renfry. ''If we have any today, looks as if you and I are elected to get it ready. They've discovered a record which shows the inside of the control board.''

''Well—that's more like it!'' Ross climbed the rest of the way into the cabin and stooped to look over Ashe's shoulder at the miniature screen. ''I'd say it's closer to the plans for a demon-inspired, four-lane thru-way,'' he commented judiciously. ''And I'll settle for a can of stew.''

Renfry and Ashe were pried away and they ate in the absent-minded fashion of men whose complete interest was centered elsewhere. When they had gone, Ross stretched and gazed at Travis.

''Care for a little look-see of our own?'' he asked with a casualness which aroused Travis' suspicion.

''In what direction?''

''That funnel place. Remember—the front hall is packed as if the boys living there had been in a hurry to move out, but had to leave their baggage behind? I'd like to have a good look at the baggage.''

''If I remember rightly, there is also a good stout grill over the doorway,'' Travis reminded him.

''And I have a way to get around that. Come on.''

Ross's way of passing the secured door was simple enough. One of the natives flew to a second-story window equipped with a coil of climbing cord from the ship. He was fronted by a shutter across the window. But prying with his spear point forced the latch on that, and a few moments later the rope dangled down the side of the building in open invitation to climb.

The gallery into which they so forced a way gave many indications it had been hurriedly stripped. Some ragged tatters of flimsy web, which fell to powder at the touch of an investigating finger, still hung on the walls. And there were pieces of oddly shaped furniture shrouded in dust. But the dust on the floor was marked in places by tracks and, seeing those, their native companion fingered his spear. Then, his eyes on the Terrans holding their attention, he drove it point down into the pattern of that trial with the vigor of one making a determined attack upon an enemy.

Another lair of the weasel things? Travis, studying those tracks in the half gloom beyond the light from the opened window, believed not. In fact, the marks were disturbingly like a human footprint. And the teasing picture provided by his imagination of some one of the old lords of this place lingering on to haunt its solitude, grew disturbingly in the back of his mind.

Here for the first time they found a stairway, though its treads were so narrow and steep as to make the Terrans believe that it had been made to accommodate bodies unlike their own. Ross, taking the lead, went down, his explorer's zeal well tempered with caution, in search of the crowded hall they had seen from without.

Travis sniffed. There was a faint fetid odor, not just the accumulation of the dust of centuries, the decay of leaves borne in by the wind, the taint of some small animal lair. This was not only strong enough to be of recent origin, but also the stench was vaguely familiar.

Warning of a weasel den? He did not think so. This was not quite so rank and compelling as that which had burdened the air in the red-walled structure those beasts had taken for their own. And it was not the alien but inoffensive odor which clung to the winged people's quarters.

He noted that the nose flap of their native companion expanded, and the deep-set eyes in that lavender face shone as they turned alertly from side to side. Not for the first time the Apache regretted the absence of a quick common form of communication. It had proved impossible for the Terrans to approximate the humming sounds which made up the natives' speech. And none of *them* in return appeared able to utter any recognizable word, in spite of all the coaxing and patient repetition of common nouns or action verbs.

The interior of the building was a grayish gloom, though the hall into which they had descended had a greater measure of light from the door. Ross stepped out, skirting a pile of boxes. He laid his hand on the top one, his other hovering over the grip of his blaster.

Travis remained where he was. That smell—it tugged at his memory. They stood still, the winged youth freezing with them. Then a sudden gust of wind puffing in the latticed doorway brought with it a warm, fresh reek and Travis knew—

"The sand people!" His words were a hiss of whisper but they carried the authority of a shout. What were the nocturnal creatures of the shrouded desert world doing here?

"You are sure?" To his surprise Ross questioned his identification no further than that.

"You don't forget a stink like that in a hurry." Travis' eyes were busy, surveying the pools of shadow about the crates and boxes piled in the hall-way. Had anything moved out there? Were they being watched now by eyes which could see farther than their own in this dusk?

The hand of the native touched his arm, an appeal for attention. Travis' head swung slowly as he saw the other ready a spear. He fitted a dart in his blow-gun.

"There is something—to the left." Ross's whisper was the thinnest trickle of sound. His blaster was pointed at that shadowy corner.

Then the hall came alive, a boiling up of forms from every likely and concealing cover. The things which beat toward them in attack shambled swiftly on four limbs like animals. Their silent advance carried with it an added horror in the fact that those slavering beasts had once been—or their remote ancestors had been—men!

The last of blaster fire crackled, brought down three of the clumsy runners. A tentacle licked out and then a fourth attacker went down, a dart dancing in its hairy throat. Behind Travis the native ran back a few steps up stairs, launched out into the air with a beat of his wings. Wheeling over the enemy, he

213

stabbed down at the boneless middle limbs raised to drag him down with a concentration which hinted at a long enmity between the two species.

Ross cried out. A tentacle flicked from the shadows, coiled about his ankle and pulled, as he fought to keep his balance. He turned the blaster beam on that rope of living flesh. He was answered by a roar as the loop fell away. Then Travis' dart caught the thing which arose to its hind legs clawing for Ross's shoulders. The Apache shot as fast as he could insert darts into the pipe. He had backed to the stairs and now he flailed out with his weapon as a club, clearing a space to drag Ross with him.

The native's spear had been jerked from his hold by a tentacle. He perched on one of the piles of boxes, and now he rocked back and forth on his refuge, beating his wings to hasten the tumble of the stack. He rose into the air just as the bulky containers crashed down across the foot of the stairway to provide the beginnings of a barrier.

"Blaster charge—exhausted," Ross panted. He gripped the barrel of the weapon now useless as a gun, smashed the butt down on the round skull of a creature scrambling over the wreckage.

They retreated up the stairway. Travis kicked out, catching another coarsely haired head under the chin, slamming its owner back and down to tangle with another eager attacker. The native sent a second pile of boxes crashing. Now he was flying back and forth over the ruck of the enemy main body, bombing them with smaller packages he snatched up from the heaps.

For a moment the Terrans were free. They took

advantage of that lull to win back to the gallery where they had entered what might have proved a trap. The native shot up, over their heads. He stood on the sill of the open window to beckon them on uttering excited hums which rose in the scale until their volume approached squeaks.

Travis shouldered Ross behind him toward the exit. "I've only two more darts—get out quick!"

For a moment the other resisted, then his common sense took command and he ran for the window. Travis aimed a dart at a hunched shoulder and head just appearing above the stairs. But that missile only nicked a furred upper arm, and fangs showed in a gap which was no longer a man's mouth. Eyes, small, red with fury, and yet alight—horribly so—with a spark of intelligence, were on him.

He backed to the window. A lavender-skinned arm reached over his shoulder, a hand fastened on the blowgun, twisted at it, trying to pull the tube from his grasp. The native still kept his post on the sill; now he wanted the weapon.

And Travis, knowing that the other had a means of escape he himself did not possess, surrendered the blowgun, then boosted his body over and out on the rope. He watched the lavender back of their rear guard. Wings projected outside the frame of the window and they were raised, ready. . . .

Then the native threw himself backward and out in a wild display of aerial gymnastics. His wings flapped wide, broke his fall and he roared again, spiraling upward as the first shaggy head protruded from the window. Hairy fists pawed at eyes which were apparently blinded by the sun. Ross had reached the ground, Travis was not far behind him. The rope swung vigorously, scraping him along the building, and he realized that those above were trying to draw him up.

The Apache let go, falling as relaxed as he could, and the lightened rope flapped wildly as it was jerked up into the window. But they were safely out in the day and he did not believe that the nocturnal creatures would pursue them into the light. However, as they crossed the strip of jungle to reach the ship, both of them applied their scoutcraft to discovering whether or not they were being trailed.

Ashe listened to their report frowningly. "It might be worse—if we were staying here."

Ross threw aside the useless blaster. "D'you mean we're getting out? When?"

"Another day—maybe two. Renfry is ready to try rewinding the tape."

For the first time Travis made himself face how much would depend upon the proper handling of that slender length of wire, how one small break would defeat their purpose and leave them exiled here forever. Or how a weakness which they could not see might develop in space, snapping their invisible tie with their home world, to set the ship drifting between solar systems an eternal derelict. *Could* Renfry rewind the spool? And if it were rewound— would it work in reverse? There could be no test flight. Once they raised ship from this spot, they were gambling with their lives on a very slender thread composed mainly of hope and an illogical belief in luck.

"You understand now?" Ashe asked. "Remember this—we can stay here."

They would be exiles for the rest of their lives, but they *would* be alive. There were enemies here, but they could set up an alliance with the winged natives, join them. Suddenly Travis got to his feet. He went to that compartment in the cabin where they had put the square of picture block which could tune in on a man's memory and make home visible to him. He had to know—whether the past had pull enough to push him into this greatest gamble of his life.

He held the slab between his hands, looked into its curdled depths. Soon he saw—red cliffs rising from the fringe of smoky green marking piñon—a blue sky—the hills of home. He could almost taste the bite of alkali dust in a rising wind, feel the swell of a horse's barrel between his legs. And he knew that he must take the chance. . . .

In the end they all made the same choice. Ross summed up their feelings:

"Time travel—that is different. We're still on our own world. If something goes wrong and we're marooned back before history began—well, it'll give a guy a bad jolt, sure. Who wants to play around with mammoths when he's more used to A-jets? But still, he'd know pretty well what he was up against and that the people he'd meet would be his own species. But to stay here—No, not even if we get the job of playing gods for the winged people! They aren't our kind—we're visitors, not immigrants. And I don't want to be a lifetime visitor anywhere!"

They made a last trip to the record library, transporting back to the ship and stowing away in every available storage place all the record tapes which appeared to be intact. The chief of the natives, delighted with the blowguns, allowed them to choose other objects from the tribe's treasure room. He only asked that they return in time, bringing with them new knowledge to share. They saw no more of the nocturnal creatures from the funnel-spired building—though they again took the precaution of sealing the ship at night.

"*Will* we be back?" Ross asked when Ashe came from his last meeting with the chief.

"Let us get home safely with this haul," Ashe returned dryly, "and someone will be back, all right. You can depend on that. Well, Renfry?"

The technician looked like a ghost of his usual self. Lines of tension, probably never to be erased, bracketed his mouth, marked the corners of his tired eyes. His hands shook a little and he could not lift his drinking container to his mouth without hooking all ten fingers about it.

"The tape's rewound," he said flatly. "And the wire didn't break. Tomorrow I'll thread it ready to run. For the rest—we pray the trip out. That's all I can tell you."

Travis lay on his bunk that night—*his* bunk, *their* ship. . . . The globe and its contents had grown progressively less alien when compared to what lay without. Around his wrist was a heavy band of red metal set with small, full, sea-green stones in a pattern which suggested breaking waves, a gift presented to him by the winged chief at their formal farewell. He was sure that the lavender-skinned flying man had not fashioned that bracelet. How old was the ornament? And from what world, from the art of what forgotten and long-vanished race had it come?

They had not even scratched the surface of what was to be found in this ancient port. Had the jungle-cloaked city been the capital of some galaxy-wide empire, as Ashe suspected? They had had no time to explore very far. Yes, there would be a return—sometime. And men from his world would search and speculate, and learn, and guess—perhaps wrongly. Then, after a while there again would be a new city rising somewhere—maybe on his own world—which would serve as a storehouse of knowledge gained from star to star. Time would pass, and that city, too, would die. Until some representative of a race as yet unborn would come to search and speculate—and guess—Travis slept.

He awoke swiftly, with a quick sense of urgency. Over his head he heard the sigh of the speaker from the control cabin.

"All ready," came Renfry's voice, thin, drained. Why, the technician must have worked through the night, eager to prove his handiwork.

"All ready."

They still had time to say "no" to this crazy venture, to choose known perils against the unknown. Travis felt a surge of panic. His hands levered against the bunk, pushing his body up. He had to stop Renfry—they must not blast into space.

Then he lay down once more, made his hands clasp the bunk straps across his body, his lips pressed tightly together. Let Renfry push the proper button—soon! It was the waiting which always wore on a man. He felt the familiar vibration, singing through the walls, through his body. There was no going back now. Travis closed his eyes and tried not to stiffen his whole body in protest against that waiting.

17

"WE'RE OUT—safely."

"So far—so good." Another voice made answer to that over the com system.

Travis opened his eyes and wondered if anyone ever became thoroughly inured to the discomfort of a planetary take-off. He had forgotten during the past days when they had been comfortably earth-bound what it meant to be wrenched into the heights beyond atmosphere and gravity. But at least the tape had worked to the extent that they had lifted safely off world.

And their flight continued, until at length they all breathed easier and began to hold more confident feelings than just hope concerning their future.

"If we simply repeat the pattern," Ashe observed thoughtfully on the evening of the fifth day, "we set down again on the desert world sometime tomorrow."

"Be better if we could eliminate that stop," Travis remarked. There was something in the desolate waste and the night things which repulsed him as nothing else had during this fantastic voyage.

"I've been thinking. . . ." Ross glanced across the swinging seat to the pilot's perch where Renfry spent most of his waking hours. "We refueled on the trip out—at the first port. Suppose—just suppose that we exhausted the supply there."

Renfry grinned, a death's-head stretch of skin across bones. His thumb jerked downward in the immemorial gesture of sardonic defeat. "Then we've had it, fella. Let's hope that we can stretch out luck past that particular point along with all the rest of the elastic tricks."

This time they downed on the desert port in the early morning, when the lavish display of flames along the horizon was paling into nothingness. They saw the blaze of the rising sun reflected too brightly from the endless drifts of sand.

"Two days here, roughly—*if* we do duplicate the pattern exactly."

Waiting two days, cooped up in the ship, not sure that they *would* take off again. At the thought of it, Travis shifted restlessly in his seat. And the specter Ross had evoked shared the narrow confines of the cabin with them all.

"Any walk-about?" Ross must be feeling it too—that goading desire to be busy, to drawn in action ever-present fears.

"Not much reason for that," Ashe replied calmly

222

enough. "We'll take a look outside—in daytime. Not that I believe there is much to see."

The sun-repelling helmets on, they opened the outer hatch. They surveyed the expanse where the winds might have whittled new patterns among the dunes, but where they could see no change since their last visit. The enigmatic sealed buildings still squatted beyond, with no sign of life about.

"What *did* they do here?" Ross's hands moved restlessly along the frame of the exit port. "There was some reason for this stop—there had to be. And why were those same things—people, animals, whatever they are—or were—on the other world, in the funnel-topped building?"

"Which are the exiles?" Ashe asked. "Is this their home world, while those others exist across the void and have for generations because they were not recalled in time? Or are these the exiles and the others are at home? We may never know the reason or answer to any questions about them." He studied the squat building among the creeping dunes. "They must live underground, with that building covering the entrance. Perhaps they live underground on the other planet also. Once they must have been here to service ships—to maintain some necessary outpost."

"And then," Travis said slowly, "the ships didn't come any more."

"Yes. There were no more ships. Perhaps a whole generation waited—hoping for ships—for recall. Then they either sank into apathy and stagnation, to slide down the hill of evolution, or they more consciously adapted to their surroundings."

"In the end, the result was the same," Ross observed. "I don't think those here are any different from the ones in the funnel building. And there they had a better world to adapt to."

"Wait!" Travis had been studying that sand-enclosed block with interest. Now he thought that his memory of the place as it had been weeks earlier did not match what he saw now. "Was that elevation on the left there before?"

Ross and Ashe leaned forward, their attention settling on the end of the structure he indicated.

"You're right, that's new!" Ross's affirmation came first. "And I don't think that projection is made of stone like the rest, either."

The block which had so oddly appeared on the corner of that distant roof did not give out a metallic answer to the sun's rays. But neither was it dull-coated. There was a sleek sheen to it, such as might be displayed by opaque glass or obsidian. The hump had no openings that they could see, and what its purpose might be remained as much of a mystery as the rest of this age-old puzzle.

It remained so for a very few moments. Then there was action of a sort the watchers in the ship did not expect. They had seen the rays which protected the roof of the building against assault or investigation. Now they witnessed the use of what must have been one of the aggressive weapons of the men who had first erected that block.

What was it which lashed out, cracked a whip's thong about the skin of the ship? A beam of fire? A bolt of energy? A force which the Terrans could neither imagine nor name?

Travis only knew that the energy wash of that blow crushed him back into the globe, hurled him into the inner door of the lock with Ross and Ashe thrust tight against him. Their bodies were flattened on the metal wall of the ship until the breath was forced from their lungs and the world went black about them.

Travis was on the floor, fighting for the air his body had to have, pain in bands about his chest. And before his blurred eyes was the open door of the port. In that moment all that mattered was that oblong of empty space—that, and beneath the torture of his body, the sense that that space must be shut out—that what lay beyond it meant final extinction.

He clawed at the body across his knees, turned over somehow and inched painfully from under its weight, moving in a worm's progress toward the outer port. There was a singing in his ears, filling his head, adding to his daze. Then he was staring out into the glare of sun and sand.

At first he thought he was lightheaded—that what he was seeing could not be true. For there was no wind, yet from the hidden floor of the landing space sand was rising in thin, unwavering sheets, walling in the globe. And those curtains of grit arose vertically, unmoved by any breeze! It was incredible—it could not happen—yet before his eyes it did.

He lunged to his knees, thrust against the door, shut out the curtains of sand, the harsh light of the sun, the thing which could not be true. And as his hands fumbled to shoot home the alien bolts, the pain lessened. He could breathe again without the constriction which had held his lungs imprisoned. He turned to the other two.

The congested blueness of their faces startled him into quick action. He jerked both men up into a sitting position against the wall. Ashe's blue eyes opened.

"What—?" He only got out that one faint word as Travis turned his attention to Ross.

There was a thin thread of blood trickling from the corner of the younger scout's slack mouth. He moaned as Travis shook him gently. Ashe moved and winced, his hands going to his chest.

"What happened?" He was able to get out the whole demand this time.

"The space—marines—landed." Ross's lips shaped the words one at a time. There was a shadow of a grin about them. "—On me, I think."

"Hullloooo down there!" The call was disembodied over the ship's com, but it was imperative. "What's going on?"

Although the hull could cut out sun, sound, the world without, they could now feel movement through its layers of protection. It was as if the ship were being buffeted by some force. Those walls of sand? Travis hauled himself to the ladder wall and began to climb, seeking the vision plate by the controls which was now their only link with outside.

He discovered Renfry standing before that link, his disbelieving eyes on thick curdles of sand, sand rising from the ground, drawing in with steady purpose to engulf the ship. They were on the point of being buried in a sea of grit, and there was no reason to believe that that was not directed, consciously, by very active animosity and intelligence.

"Can we get out?" Travis dragged himself to the nearest seat. "Any way to up ship?"

If the tape governed their departure according to the earlier schedule, they were stuck here for another night, another day. By that time the globe could be so deeply buried that there would be no hope of blasting free from the tons of sand. They would be no hope of blasting free from the tons of sand. They would be sealed into a living tomb.

Renfry's hands went out to the keyboard of the controls, hesitated there. His lips tightened.

"It's a big risk but I could try."

"It'll probably be a bigger risk to stay." Travis remembered the two he had left at the lock. They must be brought out of danger before the shock of blast-off. "Give me five minutes," he said. "Then blow—if you can!"

He found Ashe on his feet, dragging Ross out into the corridor. Travis hurried to help.

"Renfry is going to try to blast off," he reported. "We're being buried in sand."

They got Ross to a bunk. Ashe flopped into the adjoining one, and Travis barely made it to the next cabin and the waiting cushion there, when the warning shrilled through the com. There was the vibration of laboring engines. But it went on far longer than before. Travis lay tense, willing the wrench of blast-free to come, counting off seconds. . . .

The vibration was building up—higher than he had ever known it to go before. And the ship rocked on its base, movement and sound becoming one, a sickening mixture which churned the stomach, deadened thought but not fear.

The break came in an instant of prolonged red agony. Afterward came blackness—nothing at all. . . .

Vibration was gone, sound was gone—but sensation remained. And the clean, aromatic scent of the healing jelly which filled the bunks on occasion of need. Travis opened his eyes. Had they pulled free from the desert planet?

He sat up, brushing the jelly from him. It slid easily from his skin, from the suit, leaving the usual well-being of mind and body. The confidence which had been jolted out of him had already flooded back. He got to his feet, went to peer into the neighboring cabin.

Ross and Ashe still lay inert under the quivering mounds of that substance on which the aliens had based their first aid. He climbed to the control cabin.

Renfry was strapped into the pilot's chair, but his head lolled limply on his shoulders, his white face alarming Travis. A heart beat slowly under his questing fingers. He unfastened the technician, somehow managed, with the aid of no-weight, to get him to his bunk below. The vision plate presented only that swirl of dead black which was the sign of hyperspace. They had not only broken loose from the sand trap, they were also embarked on the next leg of the long journey which might or might not take them home.

How long had that portion of the journey lasted before? Nine days by Renfry's watch—nine days between the sand and the fueling port. Nine days until they could be sure that Renfry's blast-off had not thrown the tape off course.

As they recovered from that shock Ashe took command, using the loot they had gathered from the storehouse of records to focus their interest outside themselves. On the plea of hunting another ship's operation manual, he set them to work in shifts at the record reader, processing every tape which could still be run through that machine. More than one promising coil broke, whipped into a tangle they did not dare try to unravel. But even those must be kept for the experts at home to study. For Ashe never admitted after their break from the desert world that they were *not* going to get home. He pointed out that the odds they had already licked totaled a formidable sum and that there was no reason to believe that their luck would not continue to hold.

But even Ashe, Travis thought to himself, *must* have doubts, be as nervous as the rest—though he did not show it—when Renfry's watch marked the ninth day's flight and they had no warning of arrival at the fueling port. They made only a pretense of a midday meal. Travis had calculated rations just that morning. By going on very slim supplies, they would have enough of the food they dared use to see them home—*if* the voyage was not prolonged. He reported that fact to Ashe and received only an absent-minded grunt in reply.

Then—as if to prove all their worst forebodings untrue—the warning came. Travis strapped down, sharing quarters with Ross this time. The other grinned at him.

"The chief's called it right again! Here we go for a shot of gas from the service station—then home!"

Even the discomfort of landing could be forgotten when they did see about them the ruined towers marking off landing spaces, the metallic turquoise sky of their first galactic port. Why, they were almost home!

They clattered down to the space lock and opened it eagerly—to watch for the creeping snake of the fuel line and its attendant robot. But long moments went by and there was no movement in the shadow of the nearest tower. Travis studied the immediate terrain. Had they set down in the same square they had visited before? Might a change in so slight a matter provide the reason for the silence about them?

"Could be due to the time element." As Ashe's voice—sounded in his helmet com, the old man might have been reading his thoughts. "We left the second stop well ahead of our former schedule."

They clung to that hope as an hour, and then two, passed and there was no movement from the tower. Pooling their recollections of the place, they were fairly certain that they had landed in the same square. And they avoided putting into words the other dire possibility—that the mechanism of the ancient port had at last been exhausted, perhaps by the very effort put upon it weeks before when the globe had been serviced there.

Renfry spoke at last. "I don't know how much fuel we have on board. I can't even tell you the nature of that fuel. And whether we *can* take off without more is also an open question. But if we can, I don't believe we'll be able to finish the trip. We may be working against time—but we'll have to discover if we can push those machines into one more job. And we'll have to do it quick!''

They swung out of the globe, and Renfry crawled under its arching side, to discover a new catastrophe. If there had been any fuel left in the ship's sealed storage compartments, it was gone now. There was an ominous damp patch spreading from an opening at ground level.

Renfry's voice came hollowly. "That's done it, fellas. She's empty. Unless you can get that pipe line on the jog again, we're grounded for keeps.''

"What made that open up?" Ross wondered with the bafflement of one to whom machines are still mysterious save for their most obvious functions.

"Might be some mechanism triggered by this.'' Ashe stamped on the pavement. "Well, let's go and look for the robot and that animated pipe line.''

They walked toward the tower. From ground level the structure was even more pointed and needle-like. There was an opening at the foot, the doorway from which the robot had come. Ashe reached that, stood for a moment peering within.

The chunky robot which had clanked into duty at their first visit was still there, just within the doorway. And beyond, plain to be seen in a rusty, yellowish light, were a corporal's guard of its fellow. All alike, they were backed against the far wall as if awaiting some long-past official inspection.

From a well in the center of the floor, to be glimpsed around the bulk of the robot in the doorway, was a massive piece of metal which Travis recognized as the "head" of the snake pipe line.

Ashe reached out almost reluctantly to push the robot. To their surprise the machine, which had appeared so massive and immobile, answered to that handling. It did not react as might an alarm clock shaken into running once again—instead it toppled disappointingly forward with an odd flaccidity. One of the arms clattered loose and spun across the pavement to strike on the snake's head.

"It's moving! Look—it's moving!"

Ross was right. In a jerky, sullen manner the heavy end of the mobile pipe line raised, inched forward about a foot while the Terrans held their breaths in hope—until it fell supinely once more.

"Hit it again," advised Ross.

Ashe edged around the prostrate robot to inspect more closely what they could now see of the pipe. This small portion displayed no signs of deterioration. He stooped, took a good grip on the "head" and tugged. The he hurriedly jumped back while Ross and Travis kicked the robot out of the path of the creeping snake. Two feet—three—out in the open it went—and headed for the ship. Renfry saw them coming and waved, crawling back under the bulge of the globe to make ready for the pipe's arrival.

But they had exulted too soon. Some four feet away from the tower the head sank to earth once more. Ashe tried his former method of revival, without result. They took turns shaking it, together and separately. It was much heavier than the robot and they could not urge it into any further effort.

Renfry came to join in a consultation. He went

back to inspect the well from which the pipe emerged, only to return as baffled as he had gone.

"Can we pull it by hand?" Travis wanted to know.

"That's what we'll have to try now." Renfry was grim.

They brought out the light, tough rope from the ship, made fast lines about the "head," and set to work. At Ashe's word of command they gave a concentrated jerk. The stubborn pipe gave, started forward, but not under its own power. They gained another four, five feet, but the effort required to move that dead weight was exhausting. Now their gains were shorter, and the strain they must exert to produce them grew greater and greater.

Ross tripped, went down, levered himself up, his face in the bowl of the helmet showing a set snarl. He seized the rope again as if it were a man he could tangle with—and jerked in concert with the other three. This time there was no yielding at all, and their feet slipped on the cracked and age-old stone.

18

TRAVIS SAT back on his heels in the immemorial
position of the dismounted range rider. The others
sprawled beside the tow rope, their faces a congested
red from their efforts. Renfry squirmed, braced himself on his hands and began to fumble with the
latching of his helmet. He threw the bubble back and
breathed hard with the immediacy of a drowning
man.

"Put on your helmet, you fool!" Ashe raised his
head from his arms; his voice in the com was broken
by the laboring of his lungs.

But Renfry shook his head, his lips moving in
words sealed away by the protection he no longer
shared. Travis' fingers went to the fastenings of his
own helmet.

"I don't think we need these." He pulled off the

bubble and lifted his head to meet the touch of a small, playful breeze. The air was crisp, like that of a Terran autumn. And it filled his lungs in an invigorating way. He reached for the rope, ready to try again.

"There's no use in pulling ourselves blind." Ashe's voice was no longer rendered metallic by the alien com. "The trouble may lie back in the tower."

Renfry began to crawl on his hands and knees back the length of the pipe, inspecting its surface as he went. At last he staggered to his feet and lurched through the door, the others after him.

They found the technician down by the mouth of the well from which the pipe extended. He was examining the covering there, trying to wriggle the flexible tube back and forth.

"The thing must be caught—below this!" He hammered his fist against the capping.

"Can we get that lid off and see?" Ross wanted to know.

"We can try."

But such an operation required tools of a sort—levers, wedges. . . . There was the line of waiting robots—could parts of their bodies be put to more practical purposes? Ross had picked up a loose "arm," shed by the one which had disintegrated, testing the rod's strength with all the force of his own arm and shoulder.

Travis studied the well capping. There was no opening, no vestige of crack into which a wedging tool might be inserted. And now Renfry ran his hands about the ring through which the pipe issued, striving to find by touch what none of them could see. He tapped with the rod, first lightly and then with increasing force, leaving some dents and scratches, but making no other impression on the fitting.

"Does that unscrew?" Ross suggested.

Renfry scowled, spat out a couple of short and forceful words. He transferred his efforts from the immediate vicinity of the pipe to the outer rim of the cover. And it was there that he did make a promising discovery. They worked fast, one at each, to pick the accumulated dust of centuries out of four depressions in which were sunk knobs which might just be the heads of bolts.

Then they turned to the broken robot, dismantled its remains, until they were equipped with pieces of metal to force those heads. It was slow, disheartening work. Once Travis went back to the ship to gather up the containers of the jelly which had poisoned him during the testing of the supplies. They smeared the stuff in and around the stubborn knobs, hoping it would lubricate and loosen, while they pounded and prodded. But their efforts were encouraged when the first bolt yielded, and Renfry used blistered fingers to work it entirely free. And that small success gave a spurt to their labors.

It was nightfall and they were working mainly by touch when Ashe's bolt came free—the second one.

"This is it for now," he told them. "We can't rig any sort of light in here and there's no use in trying to free the rest in the dark. I've hit my fingers more than this blasted thing for the past half hour."

"Time may be running out on the journey tape," Ross answered tightly. He was putting into words one of the two fears which grinned over their shoulders during all those hours of punishing labor.

"Well, we aren't going to lift without fuel." With a sharp exclamation and a hand to his back, Ashe stood up. "And we can't work on in the the dark without rest or food. Those things we know—the rest we're just guessing at."

So they stumbled back to the ship, realizing only when they stopped the battle with the stubborn casing how completely tired they were. Travis knew that Ashe was right. They could not hope to lick the problem by driving their bodies past the point of human endurance.

They ate, more than the proper rations for the meal, wavered to their bunks, collapsing, drunk with fatigue. And Travis was still stiff in the morning when he awakened to Ross's shaking—blinking foggily up at the other's thin face.

"Back to the salt mines, brother!" Ross put the blackened and torn nail of an abused finger to his mouth. "I could do with a blowtorch now. Climb out of your downy bed, but fast, and join the slave gang."

It was midmorning before they worked the fourth and last bolt out of its bed. And for a long moment after Renfry threw it from him with emphatic force, they just sat about the rim of the well, their torn and blistered hands hanging limply between their knees.

"All right." Ashe roused. "*Now* let's see if she'll come up!"

To get levers to raise the cover they had to dismantle two more of the robots. And they carried out that destruction with a kind of savage satisfaction.

Somehow, attacking the unresisting semi-manlike forms gave them release from some of the frustration and lurking fear. They achieved stout bars and went back to attack the well cover.

They never knew afterward how long it took them to pry that plug out of its bed. But a last frantic heave on the part of all, together, suddenly snapped it apart in two halves, displaying the dark hole from which the pipe arose.

Though it was day outside, as brilliantly clear a day as the one before had been, the interior of the tower was not too well lighted and they had no torch to explore those depths.

Renfry lay down, to thrust both arms into the well, running his hands along the surface of the pipe as far as he could reach.

"Find anything?" Ashe crouched beside him, peering over one shoulder.

"No. . . ." And then he changed that to a quick and excited, "Yes!"

"I can barely touch it—feels as if the scaled coating on the pipe is caught." He wriggled and Travis caught hold of his legs to anchor him.

In the end Renfry did the rest of the tedious job painfully, with frequent halts for rest. He hung head down in that pit, kept from wedging his head and shoulders in too tightly by the others' hold on him. He had to work mainly by sense of touch, since his own body blocked out three-fourths of the already subdued light, and with improvised tools hurriedly culled from the litter about them.

The fourth time they pulled him out for a breather, he rolled over on his back and lay gasping. "I've pried the thing loose as far down as I can reach.'' His words came one by one as if he could barely summon up the strength to push them out. "And it's still fast farther down.''

"Maybe we can work it loose, pulling from up here.'' Ashe's hands curved about the scaled surface of the pipe where it projected over the side of the well.

"You can try.'' Renfry rubbed his fists across his forehead as Travis, with a heave he tried to make gentle, moved the technician's dead weight away from the side of the opening, to put his own hands overlapping Ashe's.

Together they strained to move the column of the pipe inside the tube of the well. But it appeared glued to the side where Renfry had fought to free it. Beads of sweat gathered along the line of black hair above Travis' forehead, trickled down to sting across his lips. And in the half-light he saw Ashe's jaw line set—sharp under the thin brown skin—while the cords and muscles of his arms and shoulders stood out to be modeled under the fabric of the blue suit.

Then Ross added his weight to the effort. "You pull,'' he told Ashe. "Let us push in your direction. If it is ever going to give, that ought to do it.''

For a long, long moment it seemed that the pipe was not going to give, that too much damage existed below. Then Ashe flew back, the hose striking him a forceful blow in the chest, as, out of their sight, the obstruction gave away and Ross and Travis sprawled halfway across the opening.

They scrambled up and Ross hurried to pull Ashe free of the hose. With Renfry trailing, they went back to the outer air of the port. They took up the towrope once again and began the labor of dragging the hose to meet the ship. The scaled pipe moved sluggishly, but they were winning, foot by painful foot.

Then Travis, during one of their all-too-frequent halts, glanced back and cried out. They were three-fourths of the way to their goal, but from under the belly of the hose snake was spreading a stain of moisture which gleamed in the afternoon light. That last rip to free the tube must have weakened its fabric and the burden of the unknown fuel was being lost.

Renfry stumbled back, knelt to explore, and jerked one hand away with a cry of pain. "It's corrosive—like acid." he warned. "Don't touch it."

"Now what?" Ross kicked dirt over the stain, watched the soil crumble into slime in the dark smear of fluid.

"We can get the pipe on to the ship—and hope that enough of the fuel comes through," Ashe answered in a colorless voice. "I don't think we can hope to mend the hose."

And because they could see no other way out, they went back to hauling at the towrope, trying not to glance back or think of the fuel seeping out of the pipe line. Renfry nursed his burnt hand against his chest until they at last pushed the end of the hose under the curve of the globe. He got down and crawled under, grunting with pain as he fastened the head of the snake against the opening in the ship.

"Is it feeding through?" Ross asked the all-important question.

Renfry, almost as if he dreaded the answer, put his good hand palm-down on the scaled side of the pipe, holding it there for a long moment while they waited to know the future.

"Yes."

They had no idea how much fuel the ship required—or whether the necessary amount was still available. The moist seepage along the hose continued to spread. But Renfry lay with his hand on the pipe, nodding to them from time to time that the feed of fluid was still in progress.

There came a pop like a small explosion. The head of the pipe cropped from the opening in the ship, the hose now flaccid. Renfry tapped and hammered at the cap which had slid into place, pulling down over it a second protective lock. When that clicked under his efforts he rolled out.

"That's that. We've all we're going to get."

"Is it enough?" Travis wanted to ask—to demand. But he knew that the others were as ignorant as he of the proper answer.

They straggled back to the port ladder, somehow pulled themselves up, and made their way in a blind haze of fatigue to the cabin bunks. What they could do they had done—now their success was back again in the hands of blind fortune.

Travis roused out of a dose. The vibration in the walls—They were bound off-planet again! But were they heading home? Or would that unknown fuel only take them into space, abandon them there to drift forever?

He dreamed—of red cliffs and sage, piñon pine, and the songs of small birds in a canyon. He dreamed of the feel of a desert wind against one's body and the surge of horse muscles between one's legs—of a world which was, before mankind aspired to space. And it was a good dream, so good a one that even when it drifted from him after the way of dreams, Travis lay very still, his eyes closed, trying to will it back again.

But the sterile smell of the ship was in his nostrils, the feel of the ship was under his hands, closing around his body. And his old claustrophobic dislike of the globe was reborn with an intensity he had almost forgotten. He opened his eyes with a forced effort.

"We're still on the beam." Ross sat on the bunk opposite, his face hollow with strain under the blue light. He held up his hand. Both normal and scarred fingers were crossed, and he laughed as he so displayed them. "Soup's on," he added.

They counted the ration tins again that day. The contents of those few containers must be stretched to the limit now. Ashe measured out the portions which must serve for nourishment each waking period.

"We will just have enough if the time element remains the same. Stay in your bunks as much as possible—the less energy you burn the better."

But a man could sleep just so much. And however earnestly they pursued that escape, there came a time when sleep fled and one could only lie, staring up, or with closed eyes, while lone minutes of waiting stretched into hours, always darkened by fears.

"I was thinking," Ross spoke suddenly into the silence of the cabin he shared with Travis, "when we come in we should show up on the radar screens before we land. It'll be just like some bright boy to loose off a missile, just for practice. We can't possibly signal that we're only space travelers coming home.''

''We're armed.'' But Travis wondered what defenses the globe *did* have. Missiles were top secret. Their government—other governments—could have any number of unpleasant surprises waiting to greet air-borne craft which could not adequately identify themselves.

''Dream on.'' Ross sounded scornful. ''I don't see *us* knocking down Nike Four *and* all her cousins and aunts with those cannon. We don't even know how to aim the things!''

They broke out of hyper-space, that period of discomfort heightened by their weakened condition. But in spite of that weakness, they dragged themselves to the control cabin to watch that green-patched ball grow on the vision screen. Travis discovered he was shaking, feeling almost as ill as he had during the food-testing session. Was that green ball—home? Dared they believe so—or was it a mirage they were all sharing now because they wanted it so badly? Just as the picture plate of the aliens could reproduce any man's home site to lighten his loneliness?

But now the familiar lines of the continents sharpened. Ross's head went down, his face hidden in his hands. And Ashe spoke slowly certain measured words Travis knew, though they were no part of his own heritage. Renfry's hands ran back and forth along the edge of the control board, caressingly.

''She did it! She's brought us home!''

"We aren't down yet!" Ross didn't lift his head and his words were sharp, as if perhaps he could insure their eventual safe landing by his very doubt of it.

"She brought us this far," Renfry crooned. "She'll take us the rest of the way. Won't you, old girl?"

They met the jolt of the break into Terran atmosphere, accepted it, half numbed, still unbelieving. Ross released his hold on the chair, made for the well of the ladder.

"I'm going down." He averted his eyes from the vision plate as if unable to watch any longer.

And suddenly Travis shared the other's distrust of that window on space. He followed Ross, swinging down the ladder to their cabin, throwing himself prone in the bunk to await their landing—*if* there would be a safe landing.

The thin vibration of a take-off motor was nothing to the pressure of air against the globe skin now. It raised a hum which sang in their ears, through every atom of their tense bodies. All the waiting they had managed to put behind them was nothing compared to this last stretch they could not measure by any clock. The feeling that something might—would happen—to negate all their hard-won safety gnawed deep.

Travis heard Ross mutter on the other side of the cabin but could distinguish no words. What were they doing now? Racing night or day around the surface of their world, trying to home on the spot from which the alien journey tape had lifted them weeks ago?

Seconds crawled—minutes—hours. . . . One could measure this only by uneven breaths drawn with difficulty as the weight of gravity pulled once more. Were they now registering on radar screens, hostile and friendly alike, summoning a net of missiles to fence them off from the firmness of solid earth? Travis could almost picture the rise of such a bullet trailing a spear tail of fire—coming in—

He cringed as he lay in the bunk, the soft padding rising about his gaunt body.

"Coming down."

Had those words sounded through the ship's com? Or were they only an echo of his own imagination?

He felt the pressure against the padding, the squeeze of chest and lungs, harder to bear because of his weakness. But he did not black out.

There was a jar, the ship rolled, settled slightly aslant. Travis' hands moved to the straps about him. There was complete silence. He was loathe to break it, hardly daring to move—somehow unable even now to believe that they *were* down, that under them must rest the brown soil of his own earth.

Ross sat up jerkily. Freeing himself from the protective harness of the bunk, he made for the door. He walked like a sick man, driven by some overwhelming force outside himself.

His voice came as a whisper. "Got—to—see. . . ."

And then Travis knew that he must see also. He could not accept any evidence except that of his eyes. He followed Ross along the corridor—to the inner lock. And when the other fumbled at the closing, he added his own strength to open it.

They went through the air lock, laid hold almost together on the outer port. Ross was shaking, his head hunched between his shoulders, his face gray and wet.

It was Travis who opened the door. They were facing east and the time must be early dawn, for there was a belt of shadow beneath the curve of the ship while on the horizon light banners spread pale gold. He dropped down, his eyes on that band.

"Company coming." Ross swept out an arm. There was a soaring rumble of sound. A quartet of planes in formation cut across the light patch of sky.

There were lights flashing on about the ship— flooding away the shadows. Now Travis could pick out a buckled framework, signs of a disaster. And among the wreckage men were moving, drawing in to the star ship. But beyond them the sun was rising. His sun—rising to light his world! They had made it against all the stacked odds. Travis' hand smoothed the skin of the globe beyond the frame of the open port, as he might have smoothed the arched neck of the pinto that had brought him through a grueling day's ride on the range.

The sun was yellow on the distant hills. And those were made of the good brown earth of home!

NEW YORK TIMES BESTSELLING AUTHOR
ALAN DEAN FOSTER

___ **GLORY LANE** 0-441-51664-5/$4.50

Seeth's a bored punk rocker, Miranda's an air-head beauty, and
Kerwin's a nerd who just wants to fit in. Now they're in for the
adventure of their lives—an all out space war!

___ **QUOZL** 0-441-69454-3/$4.95

They came in sleek, tastefully designed space ships. Their furry
bodies were preened to perfection, and clothed in the height of
fashion. There's never been an invasion quite like the Quozl. Earth
may never be the same.

___ **MAORI** 0-441-51925-3/$4.50

His name was Robert Coffin, but the Maori natives called him Iron
Hair. A civilized man in the raw wilderness of New Zealand, he had
come to forge a nation at the end of the world--and discovered a
magical world beyond his strangest dreams.

___ **CYBER WAY** 0-441-13245-6/$4.50

Two cold-blooded killings. All because of a Navaho sandpainting
which has mystical properties, a painting that leads to an alien data
base that defies all common sense. Detective Vernon Moody will
unearth the truth behind these killings . . . an inhuman truth.

255